CHAMP

Marcia Thornton Jones

Scholastic Inc.
New York Toronto London Auckland Sydney
Mexico City New Delhi Hong Kong Buenos Aires

To Lynne S. Brandon, Marnie Brooks,
Laurie Calkhoven, Martha Levine, Joanne Nicoll,
Becky Rector, Mara Rockliff, Susan Spain, and
Barbara Underhill. Thanks to all for your support,
encouragement, and friendship. RAH! And a special
thanks to Brantley Rosenfeld for his softball expertise!

ISBN-13: 978-0-545-00148-9
ISBN-10: 0-545-00148-X

Copyright © 2007 by Marcia Thornton Jones

All rights reserved. Published by Scholastic Inc.
SCHOLASTIC, APPLE PAPERBACKS, and associated logos are trademarks and/or registered trademarks of Scholastic Inc.

12 11 10 9 8 7 6 5 4 3 2 1   7 8 9 10 11 12/0

Printed in the U.S.A.
First printing, January 2007

Contents

1
Batter's Error

"Keep your eye on the ball, Riley," Kaylee said for the umpteenth time. With the cap pulled low over her forehead and the way she chewed a big hunk of bubble gum, she looked just like a pitcher for the major leagues.

I concentrated on smacking the ball to kingdom come. I was determined not to make a fool of myself when I went out for the Davenport Summer League. To do that, I had to get the hang of swinging at a ball going the speed of light. That's where Kaylee came in. Her aim would make Billy the Kid jealous. She was better at pitching a ball than any other fifth grader in Davenport. Especially me. Besides that, she was my best friend.

It was one of those warm March Saturdays.

The kind where the earth smells wet but the sun feels warm. It felt good to be outside. The bat was heavy in my hands and pulled at my shoulders when I gave it a swing.

"Don't forget to lead with your hips," Kaylee said. Her cap was so low over her hair that I couldn't see where she had tried to cut it herself.

"I know," I told her.

"And hold the bat high over your shoulder," she added.

"I know," I said.

"This time, wait until the ball gets to you before swinging," she said.

"I KNOW!" I yelled.

We had been practicing for nearly an hour, and this time I was sure I would hit that ball over the rooftops. I hitched my shorts up. Even with my belt on the first notch, my shorts were too big.

Since the maple tree took up most of my back-yard, we had to play baseball in the front yard. That's important to remember. It's not that we wanted to play by the street. We were even careful so that the ball would go across the yards and not anywhere near the road.

Of course, that all depended on me hitting it.

Kaylee squinted, turning her gray eyes to slits. She eyed the air between my chest and knees and then pitched the ball so hard it turned into a missile.

It was instinct that made me dodge. Balls going that fast can leave a bruise the size of Nebraska if you let them hit you. The ball sailed past me, bounced once on the grass, and ricocheted. The second bounce landed in the street.

If instinct caused me to dodge the ball, it also made me race after it. I wasn't really going to dart into the street. That's something moms and dads teach kids when they're three. But Kaylee didn't know I was going to stop at the curb. Neither did the driver.

"Riley! Watch out!" Kaylee yelled.

The driver slammed on the brakes, locking the wheels in a skid. The screeching tires scared two birds into flight.

I teetered on the curb, sneakers balancing on the edge. One foot slipped, landing in the street. That threw me off balance and I tumbled, my hands scraping blacktop.

My muscles froze when I saw the grille of the SUV, looking as big as Mount Everest, coming straight toward me.

At the last minute the SUV skidded to the left, turned a half circle, bumped over the curb, and careened off the road. The wind it created as it passed by felt cold against the sweat on my face.

The silence after the SUV crashed into the tree was worse than any sound I'd ever heard. It didn't last long.

A high-pitched wail tore through the silence. I reached the SUV just as Dad and Mom ran out of the house and across the lawn. Dad gave me a quick look before pushing me aside to open the driver's door.

"Are you okay?" Mom asked, coming up behind me. She turned me so I wouldn't see the car, but I pulled away from her grasp to watch Dad.

Kaylee ran from her pitcher's spot in the middle

of my yard to stand by me. Mom reached over to give her shoulder a squeeze.

Naturally, Mr. Douglas saw everything, too. He dropped his hoe and hurried across his front lawn. My neighbor moved pretty fast for an old man.

I was sure my next-door neighbor made a habit out of spying on my family. Nobody ever visited him, but he was always outside. He had been pretending to pull weeds from the cracks in the sidewalk that led to his front door, but I knew he was only out there so he could watch me swing the bat through the air.

A lady sat in the driver's seat, white fists clenching the steering wheel. It wasn't just any lady, either. It was Mrs. Lerner. Everybody in Davenport knew Mrs. Lerner. She lived at the base of the mountain that was named after her grandfather. She was so rich, she wore diamonds to the grocery store.

A cut over Mrs. Lerner's right eye dribbled blood, but she wasn't the one making the horrible noise. "I'm okay," she told Dad, batting his hand away from her face. "But something's wrong with the dog."

Dad flung open the back door. A wire animal carrier had slid against the far door and was wedged upside down between the seats, its metal dented and the door hanging from a single hinge. Whatever was inside howled even louder when Dad struggled to drag it out of the car. Blood splattered on Mrs. Lerner's shoes. She knelt by the cage and moaned, "Please don't let him be hurt."

Teeth bared, a border collie hunkered down in the dented kennel. Blood stained the white of his chest red. My stomach lurched when I saw a leg bone sticking out an inch above the skin.

Dad reached for me and unhooked my belt. I felt the sting as it whipped through the loops. The dog lunged for Dad's arm, but he slipped my belt over its muzzle and pulled it tight before he was bitten. Saliva dripped from the dog's mouth and its brown eyes were rimmed with white. The dog looked wildly around while Dad used his own shirt as a tourniquet to stop the bleeding. When the dog's eyes landed on me, I looked away.

"My dog!" Mrs. Lerner shrieked. "What have

you done to my dog?" Then she looked straight at me. "He's ruined! You ruined my dog!"

"It was an accident," Mr. Douglas said. For once, I was glad Mr. Douglas had been spying. It helped having someone stand up for me, especially since I couldn't summon enough spit to say a word.

"Your dog's not dead," Mom added, giving my shoulder a squeeze.

Dad stood up and wiped his hands on the back of his pants. "But he will be if we don't do something fast."

"I'll get the car," Mom told him, leaving me standing between Kaylee and Mr. Douglas.

Nobody said a word until Dad and Mrs. Lerner drove away with the dog.

"It wasn't your fault, Riley," Kaylee whispered.

I knew my father wouldn't agree. Which meant only one thing. I had disappointed him. Again.

2
Curveball

Dad didn't say a word about the accident when he got home from the vet that afternoon. Of course, all I had to do was look at Dad to know he blamed me. Dad expected perfection. He didn't demand it. He didn't command it. He expected it. When I wasn't perfect, I could tell by the crease on his forehead.

Mom sat on the edge of my bed that night and tried to tuck me in like I was four years old. I wouldn't let her smooth my brown hair off my forehead either.

"The dog will be okay," she said. "It was just a terrible accident. You can't blame yourself."

"Is that what Dad said?" I asked, and even I must admit my voice wasn't polite.

Usually Mom would get after me for talking like that. She didn't take any sass. This time Mom glanced to the open bedroom door, making sure Dad wasn't eavesdropping. "Nobody blames you, Riley. Now, go to sleep. Things will be better in the morning. They always are."

Mom turned out the lights, but that didn't mean I fell asleep. Every time I closed my eyes, I remembered how Mrs. Lerner's dog's eyes had locked on mine. My mind buzzed with what-ifs. What if Kaylee and I hadn't been playing in the front yard? What if I hadn't missed the ball? What if I hadn't fallen off the curb? What if Mom and Dad had more than one kid? What if Kaylee was Dad's kid instead of me? What if I'd never been born? What if?

I finally turned on the light and tried reading, but the words blurred on the page. I stared at the Escher print on my wall. I could look at that drawing for hours, trying to follow the shapes and patterns that twisted and turned on one another like a maze. Tonight, even that got old.

When my bedsheets were knotted and damp

with sweat, I finally got out of bed to work on my bridge.

Our teacher, Mr. Patrick, had done an economics unit in the fall. Each group had to design and build a toothpick bridge within a certain budget. Our group decided to build the simplest kind of bridge, thinking it would be cheapest. It was, but it was also one of the weakest. When Mr. Patrick hung weights from the center, it was the first to collapse.

Since then, I had been trying to build a suspension bridge, one of the hardest to make. It was slow work, but I didn't care. I liked the idea that tiny slivers of wood could, together, form a structure that spanned distance and supported the weight of the sky.

Gluing toothpicks didn't get my mind off the accident like I thought it would. "It's not my fault," I mumbled as I dabbed glue on a toothpick. "It's not my fault," I said when I held the toothpick in place. No matter how many times I said the words, they didn't feel any truer.

I worked on the bridge until the night sky lightened and then finally grew bright with the rising sun. I heard Dad get up and bang coffee mugs around in the kitchen. I heard the front door open and close when Mom brought in the newspaper. Still, I sat and glued. One toothpick after another. That's where I was when Kaylee knocked on my door. She carried a bat slung over her shoulder the way a soldier carries a rifle.

"A bunch of us are riding our bikes over to the empty lot on Snyder Street for a pickup game. Let's play ball!" She shouted that last part, pretending to be a sports announcer. That was so Kaylee. We had basically grown up together since her father and my father had been best friends before her dad died from some terrible disease. Just because I'd seen her almost every day of my life, it didn't mean we were anything alike. I knew she had already forgotten the accident.

Not me. The thought of swinging a bat at empty air was the last thing I wanted to do. "I'm busy," I told her.

"Come on," Kaylee said. "You can work on your bridge later. Besides, you won't get better if you don't practice."

She sounded just like my dad. Practice, practice, practice. That's what he always told me, and when it came to sports, my dad knew what he was talking about. After all, he intercepted the ball and ran ninety-five yards for the winning touchdown on homecoming night when he was a senior at Davenport High. People still talk about it as if he had just snatched that ball out of thin air to run under the goalposts.

That's one of the good things about living in a small town. People remember when you do something right. Of course, it works the other way, too. They never forget when you do something stupid, either.

Like the time last fall when I made a soccer goal. My first and only goal of the season. Too bad I kicked it into our team's net. Dad had been so embarrassed he hadn't talked to me until we were halfway home.

Mom didn't seem to think it was any big deal.

Shows how much she knew. "It's not whether you win or lose," she had said in a sing-songy voice on the ride home. "It's how you play the game."

I had caught Dad's eyes in the rearview mirror. I looked away, but not quick enough. "Yeah?" I mumbled. "Try telling that to Dad, why don't you?"

"I don't expect you to win every game you play, Riley," Dad had said. "You'll do better next time."

Dad would never give up hope that his one and only kid would follow in his footsteps and become a sports superhero. "There isn't going to be a next game," I had said as he pulled onto our street that night. "I quit."

Dad sighed. "How many times do I have to tell you, Riley? Nobody likes a quitter."

He had said the exact same thing after I quit the track team in fourth grade, but my dad ate, breathed, and talked nothing but sports. I knew that he'd be disappointed if I didn't play something. So this year, I picked the perfect sport. Baseball. I'd watched enough baseball on television to know that most of the time you just stood around chewing gum.

But Kaylee was right. If I didn't practice, I'd be the number one strikeout king of the Davenport Summer League. And that would mean another disappointment to my dad.

I found my mitt buried in a tangle of socks and underwear on the closet floor. I slipped it on and punched my fist into the leather like I'd seen players on television do. Then I met Kaylee out back. She was perched on her bike, ready to take off.

"It's about time," she said in a whisper as soon as I rolled my bike out of the garage. "That man is giving me the creep-olas."

I didn't have to ask who she meant. Mr. Douglas was out in his garden again.

Sometimes I wondered if Mr. Douglas ever went inside. He always seemed to be in his yard pinching blooms, trimming leaves, pulling weeds. Pretty amazing his plants weren't whittled to stubs with all the attention they got. If he wasn't in the garden, then you could pretty much bet he'd be sitting on the old swing out under the maple tree in his backyard. I knew the real reason he was outside so much. He was looking in our yard. Watching.

Mom saw nothing strange about the old man who lived next door. She would tell me how Mrs. Douglas started the garden and how sweet it was that Mr. Douglas tried to keep it going ever since she died. Of course, I was just three when Mrs. Douglas died and didn't even remember what she looked like. Mom always got dreamy-eyed when she talked about how Mr. and Mrs. Douglas would sit in that old swing and hold hands. She could remember when Mr. Douglas had built it for his wife as an anniversary present. Whenever Mom talked about Mr. Douglas, she used words like *kindly, interesting,* and *lonely.* She never mentioned the truth: *nosy.*

"Every time I come over, that man is standing there and staring," Kaylee said. "It's not natural."

"You should try being his neighbor," I muttered.

"Living next door to a geriatric spy is not my idea of a good time," Kaylee said as she pushed off and pedaled down the driveway that separated our house from Mr. Douglas's fence. "Race you to the Snyder lot!" she called over her shoulder.

I hung my mitt on the handlebars and hooked my foot in the pedal, pretending Mr. Douglas was nothing more than a figment of my imagination. It didn't work.

"Heading out for a little baseball practice?" he asked over his pruning shears.

I knew to never, ever make eye contact with someone the age of your grandparents. They take it as an open invitation to do things like pinch your cheeks and pat your head. I kept my eyes glued to the front tire spokes and nodded.

"Thought you were a soccer player, through and through? Saw you kicking that black and white polka-dotted ball last fall."

I tried thinking of a way to answer him without actually speaking but realized it couldn't be done. "I don't play soccer anymore," I told him honestly. I didn't start pedaling so I wouldn't seem too rude, but I still refused to look up at him. I concentrated on the thorns of one of his rosebushes instead. "I'm playing baseball now."

"I see," Mr. Douglas said, though I couldn't imagine what he saw at all.

"I have to go practice," I added and got ready to ride away.

"What happened to that dog?" Mr. Douglas blurted out the question so it hung in the air, as sharp as the blades of the shears in his hand. "Is he going to live?"

It was bad enough that he was forever spying on my family. Now Mr. Douglas had the nerve to open his mouth and bring up the one subject I didn't want to think about. He stood there, pruning shears poised in midair, waiting for me to answer.

I looked up before I could stop myself. "Of course he's going to live," I said. "He just broke a leg."

Mr. Douglas shrugged. "I wasn't sure. After all, that's a show dog. One of Mrs. Lerner's champions that she's forever bragging about."

He was making absolutely no sense. I wondered if he'd suddenly gotten one of those diseases that affect people's brains and make them say crazy things.

"Show dogs are serious business," Mr. Douglas

went on. "That dog of hers meant good money for her Lerner Mountain Kennels. If he can't show and he can't breed, he's not much use to her. Folks like Mrs. Lerner would just as soon put a dog down rather than pay the vet expense."

Then Mr. Douglas bent down to snip the wilted blooms off an azalea bush as if I wasn't even there. As if he hadn't just thrown me a curveball.

3

Strikeout King

Mr. Douglas's words seemed to chase me down the driveway. "It wasn't my fault," I said to the trees blurring by. Kaylee was long gone, so I slowed my pedaling. "It wasn't my fault. It wasn't my fault." Saying the words still didn't help.

Cooper Street wasn't the way to get to the lot on Snyder. I made the turn anyway.

Cooper was lined with oak trees that arched over the street. The longer I stayed on Cooper, the bigger the houses got. They all seemed to lead to the last house at the base of Lerner Mountain. It was the biggest one in town. An estate is what most people called it. And everyone knew who lived there. Mrs. Lerner.

Mom told me the Lerners once owned half of

Davenport, but Mrs. Lerner had sold it off, bit by bit, until all that was left was the house sitting on a lot big enough to build a department store on. It was an old house with a front porch that stretched around two sides, but there weren't any rockers or swings on it. Mrs. Lerner was not the type to have a porch party.

I propped my bike against a tree and walked slowly along the wrought-iron fence until I came to a sign that said LERNER MOUNTAIN KEN-NELS. Her dog wasn't in the yard, and I didn't see his nose pressed against any windows. In fact, there wasn't a dog to be seen, but I knew they were around from the barks and yelps coming from two long buildings that formed a right angle at the far end of the property.

Behind the buildings, the mountain rose so that the kennels themselves were softened by shadows. They were simple rectangular buildings surrounded by chain-link fences. From where I stood, I could barely make out several dogs running back and forth, back and forth. I knew none of them was the one from the accident. They were moving too freely and weren't favoring a front left leg.

"Just because I don't see the dog, it doesn't mean a single thing." I hoped saying it out loud would make it sound more real. "The dog could be snoring away in a little doggy basket next to Mrs. Lerner's bed."

Somehow, though, I didn't believe it.

"It's not my fault," I mumbled in time to my pedaling as I rode away. "It's not my fault. It's not my fault."

Kaylee and some kids from the neighborhood were waiting when I finally pedaled my way to the lot on Snyder Street. "What took you so long?" Kaylee asked.

"We thought you might be playing in the street again," Frank said. That was just like him to make a joke first thing. It wasn't funny. I ignored him when he crossed his brown eyes and stuck out his tongue.

"Glad to see you're in one piece," Luke said. If that were coming from anyone else I would've thought he was poking fun at me, but I knew Luke was serious. He was serious about everything. Even about the way he looked. I never saw him with his blond hair out of place or his shirttail untucked.

Caitlin, on the other hand, was never serious. "We don't need any squashed players," she said.

"It's not like it would be a big loss or anything," Erica said.

Erica always stood tall and proud, but she never smiled. At least, not at me. It wasn't a secret that she didn't like me. There was a moment when nobody said a word.

"And losing is exactly what will happen if we don't practice," Kaylee said, breaking the silence. It bothered me that she didn't try to explain what had really happened. That the accident hadn't been my fault at all.

Frank nodded. "Everyone make sure Riley doesn't play in the street anymore and we'll be fine. Lesson number one: The baseball diamond," he said very slowly, as if he were talking to a three-year-old, "is in the grass. Not in the street."

I knew they were just kidding around, but I didn't have to like it. "I wasn't playing in the street," I told them all. It came out snippy, but I didn't care.

"We know," Luke said. "Kaylee told us before you got here. Are we all ready to play ball? We have a lot of work to do if we're going to be the best Davenport team that ever existed."

And that was that. The ribbing was over. At least for a while. We split into two teams. Kaylee and I were on the same team. I figured that evened out the odds a little. Erica was on the other team, which was fine by me.

Being on a baseball team wasn't bad. I didn't mind playing right field. Hardly anyone hit the ball my way, but when they did I had no trouble shielding the sun with my mitt and waiting for the ball to drop. No, catching a ball was not the problem.

Batting was my weakness. So far I'd hit the ball once when I got up to bat. It was a foul but, still, I hit it. Other than that, I'd swung through nothing but air.

Erica stood at first base and took the tone of a

radio announcer when it was my turn at bat. She held her hand to her mouth as if she grasped a microphone. "The strikeout king stands at home plate," Erica announced to the world. "Swing, batter, batter, batter, batter, batter," she sang.

Sweat collected on my upper lip as I held the bat over my right shoulder. Frank wound up his pitch, then let it fly. "Keep your eyes on the ball," Kaylee yelled.

What good does saying something like that do? Just because I was looking at a speeding missile didn't mean I could hit it. I proved my point by swinging so hard I nearly fell down.

"Strrrr-ike one," Erica announced to the world.

"Don't let her get to you," Kaylee told me. That did about as much good as telling a baby not to listen to the booms during the Fourth of July fireworks.

I tightened my grip on the Louisville Slugger and waited for Frank to throw the next pitch. "Swing, batter, batter, batter, batter," Erica called to the tops of the tree branches. I turned to tell her to shut up. Unfortunately, that's exactly when

Frank threw the ball. I didn't see it coming until it was too late. The ball smacked into the mitt of the catcher.

"Strrr-ike two!" Erica cried in a delighted voice.

I wasn't going to give Erica the joy of seeing me strike out. I dropped the bat to the ground and watched it bounce once before rolling to a dead stop.

"Don't give up," Kaylee told me, walking up to me. "Ignore her. She's just being a typical pain in the butt."

I took a deep breath, not liking the way it shook. "I've had enough," I told Kaylee. "I'm leaving."

"You always quit," Kaylee shouted after me.

"You sound just like my dad," I told her.

"Well, maybe your dad is right," Kaylee said.

I couldn't believe my best friend had said that. She knew how tough my dad was on me. She, of all people, knew.

I kicked the bat to one side as I strode toward my bike. I felt everyone's eyes on me as I walked past Erica.

"Must be tough," Erica said, "knowing that your girlfriend is a better athlete than you."

"Shut up," I said between clenched teeth. I wanted to reach out and push her. Nothing would've suited me better than to see her land in the dust. But I didn't do it. Not me. Instead, I grabbed my bike and raced back down Snyder.

I didn't stop until I reached my room. Didn't stop to talk to Mr. Douglas when he yelled hello. Not to put my bike away in the garage. Not even when Mom yelled to quit slamming the door.

My room was my fort in the middle of a war zone. Safe and secure. It held everything I needed. Bed. Shelves with books and toys. Escher posters plastered on the wall. A desk where I was building my bridge.

I sat at my desk and took several deep breaths until my heart slowed down. Then I unscrewed the lid on the glue jar and placed the next toothpick in line with the last. I concentrated on lining up the toothpicks. I pushed all other thoughts out of my mind. I didn't think of anything else. Not baseball. Not winning. Or losing. Not about the screeching tires or the sound that dog had made. Not the sight of jagged bone pushed through bloody skin. Not about how Kaylee thought I was a quitter. Just like my dad did. No. I didn't think of anything except making sure each toothpick was straight.

I was still gluing toothpicks when Dad knocked on my door. I hadn't even heard his car pull into the driveway.

"Mind if we talk, Riley?" Dad asked. He held my glove. I'd left it lying in the middle of the yard, along with my bike.

It was never good when my dad started a conversation that way. I carefully let go of the toothpick, making sure it was firmly in place. Then I shrugged. It's funny how parents can take a shrug to mean anything they want. Today, he decided it meant I wanted to listen to what he had to say.

Dad rubbed his hand over my mitt. "If you took better care of your equipment," he said, "it would last longer."

I didn't say anything. I didn't need to.

"The sun will dry out the leather," Dad went on as if I cared. "Rubbing in saddle soap is good

27

for the leather. I'll show you later. Then maybe I can pitch a couple of balls and help you with that swing of yours. Besides, it'll do you good to get out of this room. You spend too much time on arts and crafts."

For the first time I glanced up and caught Dad's eyes. "My bridge isn't a craft," I told him.

Dad didn't look convinced, but he changed the subject. "I talked with Mrs. Lerner today," he said. "She's very upset."

My face got hot and my stomach suddenly felt like an anthill had taken up residence right above my belly button. "I wasn't going to go out in the street," I said. "Really I wasn't."

"That's not what Mrs. Lerner believes," Dad said, but I knew what he really meant. *He* didn't believe it. "It wouldn't hurt for you to apologize to her."

"It wasn't my fault," I argued. "I stopped on the curb. I didn't do anything wrong."

Dad took a deep breath. "Show dogs are valuable," he said. "She had a lot of money wrapped up in that dog."

"Her dog didn't die," I pointed out.

Dad's hand rubbed at the deep crease in his forehead and then it fell to my desk, absently picking up a couple of toothpicks. He tapped the toothpicks' pointy ends on the base of my bridge. "Her dog may not survive, Riley. Dogs like that have to be perfect or they won't win competitions. Mrs. Lerner has no use for a crippled dog."

I was wondering what a person does with a broken show dog. Do they sell it? Give it away? I didn't have to wonder for long. Dad told me.

"Mrs. Lerner might have him put to sleep, and she believes it's all because you were playing in the street. You owe her an apology. A *big* one. You don't want Mrs. Lerner mad at you."

I felt like Dad had sucker-punched me. He was talking about killing a dog because of a broken leg. How was that my fault? I couldn't see the sense in getting rid of something just because it wasn't perfect. Then it hit me. In Dad's eyes, I wasn't perfect, either.

"Mrs. Lerner had some good points, Riley," Dad said. "If you hadn't been so close to the street she wouldn't have swerved to avoid hitting you. All I'm asking is that you apologize. Tell her you're sorry for causing her to hit that tree."

I stared at my dad as if he'd just grown broccoli for ears. He cared more about Mrs. Lerner's feelings than his own son's.

When I didn't say anything, Dad nodded as if everything had been decided. "Now, how about working on this glove? We'll get it in tip-top shape before you sign up for Summer League. Then I'll toss a couple balls your way and we can work on that swing."

"I don't care about that glove, and I don't want to play baseball, either," I said. "I want to work on my bridge."

"It'll be fun, Riley. You and me, playing ball together." Dad tossed the toothpicks on my desk. Two of them rolled off the edge and landed on the floor right before he reached for my shoulder to give it a squeeze. "Why sit up here all day when you could be out in the fresh air hitting a few balls? Don't you want to get better?"

The ants in my belly were racing in circles. They grew and swelled. Dad had no idea what it took to build a bridge. He didn't consider the time and concentration. He didn't care. All he wanted was for me to be a sports jock. Like he had been.

Those blasted ants in my belly made me do it. I picked up a dictionary and slammed it down in the center of my bridge, smashing weeks of work to smithereens. Toothpicks snapped and scattered.

"There," I told Dad. "Are you happy now?" I kept my voice low and even so he couldn't say I was being sassy.

The way Dad jumped back nearly made it all worthwhile. "Oh, Riley," he said. "What were you thinking? Maybe we can fix it."

I shook my head. "It can't be fixed," I told him as I swept the shattered bridge into the wastebasket. "This can never be fixed."

4
Champ

There are days when school seems to last for-ever. The day after trashing my bridge was one of those days.

"What's wrong with you?" Kaylee asked as soon as the bell rang.

Kaylee and I only lived three blocks apart and usually walked home from school together, but today I had decided I wasn't going straight home. There was something I needed to find out. "Nothing," I lied.

"Don't be mad about yesterday," Kaylee said. "I shouldn't have said that about your dad."

I shrugged. What else could I do?

"He isn't all that bad, you know," Kaylee said softly.

"That's easy for you to say," I told her. "You don't live with him. Even if you did, it wouldn't be so bad since you're good at every sport you try. You should've been his kid instead of me."

Kaylee matched my steps for half a block without saying a word. "That's not true and you know it," she finally said. "I know you don't get along with him, but at least you *have* a dad, Riley."

Immediately, I felt bad right down to my toenails. Kaylee's father had been dead so long, sometimes I forgot about it.

"I'm sorry," I said. "Dad just gets on my nerves. I think he's sorry he ever had me."

Kaylee suddenly grinned. "Thinking'll get you in trouble every time," she said. "So let's stop thinking about all this downer stuff and go hit some balls."

It would've been easy to say yes. To go home and swing at the ball. Lots easier than what I was planning. "Can't. There's something else I need to do."

As usual, Kaylee was all questions. She didn't keep secrets from me, and I didn't keep them from her. I thought about making this my first secret, but she wouldn't stop bugging me until she got it out of me. "You can't tell anyone," I warned.

Kaylee bounced on the balls of her feet, her eyes wide as if she'd spotted Santa Claus. "Cross my heart and hope to die," she said.

"I'm going to check on that dog," I said. "See what happened to him."

Kaylee's smile drained from her face. "Are you sure that's a good idea, Riley? Maybe you should leave well enough alone."

"I can't," I told her. "I have a bad feeling about all this. I need to see that he's okay."

Kaylee's face erupted into her usual smile again. "Let's do it, then."

I couldn't help smiling. That was just like Kaylee. Always ready to go.

A cold wave of air slapped us in the face when we opened the door to the veterinarian's office. A too-clean odor permeated the office, the kind of smell meant to hide things. From behind a closed door, a dog's deep bark ended with a whine that sounded like a question.

"May I help you?" a lady wearing heavy glasses asked from behind a counter. A badge on her collar said *Sydney*.

Sydney's eyes looked big through her glasses. She stared at us with raised eyebrows. Waiting.

"We came to see the dog," I said.

"I beg your pardon?" Sydney asked.

"The dog." I blurted it so loudly, the words echoed through the office. "I came about the dog."

Sydney's eyebrows arched a little bit higher. "What dog?" she asked. "We happen to have more than a few today."

Kaylee was right. This was not one of my brightest ideas. I had no business being here, asking about a dog that belonged to someone else. No business at all.

I was ready to bolt. It would have been easy to turn, pull open the door, leave the chilled antiseptic air, and run. But I didn't. I stood there, took a breath. "Mrs. Lerner's dog," I said.

"I want to know about the dog that Mrs. Lerner owns."

Sydney's eyebrows shot up so high, they disappeared in the tangled bangs scattered on her forehead. "And why is that?" she asked.

My mouth opened and closed, but no words came out. I knew I stood there looking like a goldfish. I would've still been standing there if it hadn't been for Kaylee.

"We're neighbors," Kaylee explained. She wasn't really lying. Since Kaylee lived three blocks away from me, she and I were neighbors, but I knew she meant for Sydney to believe we were Mrs. Lerner's neighbors. "We sort of know the dog and we're worried about him."

Sydney looked long and hard through her thick glasses. "He's this way," she finally said. She turned and led us down a hall without even checking to see if we were following. At the end of the hall was a heavy wooden door. Sydney pulled it open.

The back room was lined with wire cages. In the center was a stainless-steel table. The vet hovered over a far counter, jotting notes on paper. Sydney cleared her throat, waiting for him to look up. A question was in his eyes, but he didn't ask it.

"These kids want to see that show dog of Mrs. Lerner's," she told the vet. As soon as she released the words, Sydney disappeared back through the door.

The vet adjusted his glasses on his nose. The silver frames matched his hair. He held out his hand for me to shake. "Dr. Fayette," he told us even though we already knew that since his name was painted on the glass door of the office.

"Riley," I told him. "Riley Walters. And this is my friend Kaylee Townsend."

Dr. Fayette shook both our hands. Then he looked back at me. "Walters. I know that name," he said.

I barely nodded. "My dad is Joe Walters. The football player." That's all I usually had to mention for people's faces to smile in recognition. Dr. Fayette smiled like all the others, but his words surprised me.

"I remember the name now," Dr. Fayette

said. "He's the one that brought in the dog after the accident. Didn't realize your dad was a football man."

I felt my face redden, but Dr. Fayette didn't seem to notice. "Champ is right back here. I'll show you."

"Champ?" Kaylee asked.

Dr. Fayette grinned. "That's not his real name. But saying Champion Lerner Mountain's Spirit Captain is a mouthful."

"That's a dumb name for a dog," I said.

Dr. Fayette laughed. "I couldn't agree with you more. Most show dogs have ridiculous names."

Dr. Fayette led the way to the corner cage in the back of the room and held out his hand as if he were introducing us to his grandmother. "Here he is."

Champ sat up in the cage. The cage was high off the ground. Level with my eyes. The white on his chest seemed a little grayer than I remembered, and I noticed the hair under his chin was knotted. When he looked at me, his tail swept across the stainless steel.

"Look at that," Kaylee said. "He likes you!"

Dr. Fayette laughed. "This dog is a sweetheart. He likes anybody who'll give him attention."

I didn't look long at Champ's tail, eyes, black nose, and panting tongue. Instead, I stared at where his left front leg should have been.

"He's doing well," Dr. Fayette said. "Gaining strength. He has a great appetite and doesn't need as much pain medicine today. Seems to have adjusted to three legs just fine. Most dogs do. In fact, I think he'll be ready to go home in a few days. I'm just waiting for Mrs. Lerner to decide what she wants to do with him."

"Do?" Kaylee asked.

I only half-listened. When I glanced up, I caught Champ staring right back at me. His eyes were different from the day of the accident. They seemed brighter and calmer. I reached my fingers through the cage and let the dog lick my fingertips.

Dr. Fayette opened the cage door and the dog stood, balancing on his three remaining legs. He step-hopped closer to the edge. Dr. Fayette moved aside so I could get closer.

Champ nosed my neck and leaned against me, letting my shoulder take some of his weight. I scratched his neck and tried to listen to Dr. Fayette.

The dog, content, rested his chin on my shoulder. That's how we were when the door swung open and Sydney reappeared. Mrs. Lerner was right behind her.

There have been lots of times when I wished I could be invisible. Those other times were nothing compared to how I felt just then.

The air in the office changed as soon as she came in. Everything became tense and serious. Mrs. Lerner gave the impression that she had more important places to be. I noticed that Champ's tail sped up at the sight of her. If she noticed, she didn't care.

Mrs. Lerner didn't look at Kaylee or me. She glanced in the cage. "I can't believe this," she said. "It's such a waste." I was surprised to see tears fill her eyes, but they didn't spill over. She blinked them away.

Dr. Fayette scratched behind Champ's ear. "He

can still lead a normal life," Dr. Fayette said. "Once he recuperates."

Mrs. Lerner shook her head. "I'm not in the business of playing nursemaid to wounded animals," she said. "He can't show, and no one wants puppies bred from a three-legged dog. I've thought long and hard on this and I've decided to settle my bill. What will it cost to put him down?"

My fingers caught in the fur around Champ's neck. I was glad the dog didn't know what Mrs. Lerner was talking about.

Kaylee had been quiet until then, but that sure got her sputtering. "Put him down? You mean, kill him? Why?" Kaylee blurted. "You can't just kill him."

"I can do anything I want, young lady," Mrs. Lerner pointed out. "He is my dog."

Something about the way Champ watched Mrs. Lerner, as if he expected to get a doggy biscuit, bothered me. I recognized that look. It was trust.

"He earned that champion title," I said. "He

41

worked hard for you. How can you just forget about all that?"

"I won't forget," Mrs. Lerner said, her voice a little softer. "He's been a good dog. A grand dog. But what good is he now? There is no place for a three-legged dog in a show ring. Putting him out of his misery is the kindest thing to do."

"Wait," I said without thinking. "Let me have him."

The words surprised me as much as everyone else.

"Don't be a fool," Mrs. Lerner said. "You could never afford his medical expenses."

She was right. All I had to my name was twenty-seven dollars and eighty-three cents. Not enough.

Dr. Fayette cleared his throat. "I could work something out with Riley," he said. "If he's really serious, he could work off the expense cleaning cages after school."

"I'll do it," I said. Just like that, the words were out of my mouth.

Mrs. Lerner looked from Dr. Fayette to me.

"What could you possibly want with a three-legged dog?" she asked. "Don't you see? He's useless."

Mrs. Lerner sounded totally confused. I knew why. In her eyes, Champ was too much trouble because he wasn't perfect. But I knew all about not being perfect.

I remembered how my dad wanted me to tell her how sorry I was, but sorry was the last thing I felt just then. I didn't apologize. No, sir. I looked Mrs. Lerner straight in the eyes.

"Champ isn't useless," I said. "Give me a chance, and I'll prove it."

5
Guts

"That was totally cool, Riley," Kaylee said. "Did you see the look on Mrs. Lerner's face? It couldn't have been more pinched if she had bitten into a pickle the size of a watermelon."

Kaylee hadn't stopped talking since we'd left Dr. Fayette's office, which was fine by me since I didn't have enough spit to say anything, anyway.

"Having a dog will be great," Kaylee went on. "I always wanted a dog. Mom said she doesn't have the time for a pet. Or the money. Boy, I wish I had a dog, too."

"I'm as good as dead," I finally said. "When my parents find out, they will kill me."

Kaylee shook her head. "As soon as they get used to the idea, they'll be fine."

"Maybe Mom," I said. "But not Dad."

When Kaylee didn't answer, I knew she thought so, too.

I couldn't wait to work up enough courage to face my parents. I had to tell them the next morning, because Dr. Fayette was expecting a letter from Mom or Dad saying it was okay if I brought Champ home. He also expected me right after school to start working off the expenses.

I planned it just right. I waited until I'd slung my backpack over my shoulder to leave for school. Mom was watering the African violets that lined every one of our windows. Dad was putting on his shoes. Dad works for the Davis Heating and Cooling Company and had to be there early. Everybody was busy, not really paying attention to anyone else.

"By the way," I said as if it were nothing, "I won't be coming straight home after school."

"Going to practice your swing?" Dad asked without looking up from his shoelaces.

"Not today. I told Dr. Fayette I'd help him out at the office, but I need a note saying it's okay."

There it was. Out in the open. I put a piece of paper and a pen on the kitchen counter. Mom sat the watering can by the sink and eyed the piece of paper as if it were something I'd dug out from under my toenail. Dad looked up, that crease forming between his eyes.

"Isn't Dr. Fayette the vet?" Dad asked.

I nodded.

"You're too young for a job, Riley," Mom said.

"It's not really a job," I told her. "I'm helping out. Just for a while. To help with Champ's expenses."

"Champ?" Mom asked.

"Mrs. Lerner's dog," I said as if that explained everything.

For the briefest of moments I thought Dad was going to smile. "You talked to Mrs. Lerner?" he asked. "And apologized?"

"Not exactly," I said. This was the hard part. The whole-truth-and-nothing-but-the-truth part. I spit it out fast so Mom or Dad didn't have a chance to squeeze in a word. "She was going to put Champ

46

down so I told her I'd take him. Bring him home. Prove he wasn't useless. Dr. Fayette is letting me work off the vet bill, but he needs a note from you first." I nodded toward the paper lying on the counter.

There it was. Nothing to do but ride out the storm.

"A dog?" Mom said. "You said you'd take that dog without asking us first?"

"Champ is a trained show dog," I said with a whoosh of air. "He won't be any trouble once he learns to get around on three legs. I'll keep the dog hair off the furniture and clean up his messes in the yard. I promise."

"If you wanted a dog, you should have said something before. We could've gone to the pound and gotten a dog that was healthy and fit," Dad said.

"I think it's great you want to help out," Mom added. "But you should've asked first. A dog is a big responsibility. Are you sure you're willing to come home right after school every day to take him for walks? And to wake up early every morning to take him out before school? Remember, a dog isn't like a hamster."

I'd never really had a pet before. Not unless you counted a goldfish named Fred and the hamster I called Rat. Fred went belly-up in two days so I didn't consider him much of a pet. Rat lasted a little longer, by about a week. I left the cage door open one day, and Rat escaped through the front hall. It wouldn't have been such a bad thing except Mom opened the front door to get the newspaper. Rat skittered straight between her legs, heading for wide-open space. Mom didn't stop screaming for a full twelve minutes, which I actually thought was pretty cool but was smart enough not to say so. Didn't dare.

"I'm older now," I said. "I'll make sure Champ doesn't run between your feet." I couldn't help giving a little smile.

Mom gave me a dirty look, but she didn't say anything. Dad looked like he was ready to open his mouth, so I talked fast before he had a chance.

"You don't understand," I said. "You didn't see the way Champ's eyes watched every move Mrs. Lerner made. You weren't there when she decided to just put him to sleep because he wasn't perfect anymore. I didn't have time to talk to you first because Mrs. Lerner was going to kill him then and there. I had to act fast. I had to save Champ," I said. "I had to."

"You really believe that?" Dad asked.

I nodded, afraid to say anything else.

Mom put her hands on my shoulders. "I'm proud of you," she said.

"You are?" I squeaked.

"You're taking a stand for something you believe in," she said.

"That took guts," Dad said. "It shows initiative."

If one of Mom's African violets had reached out and swallowed the refrigerator, I wouldn't have been more surprised. If Dad actually thought what I did was a good thing, then maybe, just maybe, everything would work out.

I should've known better.

Dad finished tying his other shoe and put his foot down on the linoleum. It landed with a thud. "But a dog is a huge responsibility, Riley. It isn't like soccer, where you can sign up to play and then quit the next week."

It was just like Dad to relate everything I did back to how bad I was at sports.

I pulled open the back door and the paper on the counter floated to the floor and landed by my dad's feet.

"If I could, I'd take back ever trying to hit that stupid baseball." I started out low, but my words bubbled and swelled until they filled the kitchen. "Then the accident wouldn't have happened and Champ would still be winning his blue ribbons. But I can't change it. I can't change a thing. I just thought I could keep things from getting worse. You won't even let me do that, so because of you Champ will die and everyone will say it's my fault!"

I slammed the door behind me. I was halfway across the yard when I heard Dad yelling. "Riley," he said. "Do not storm out of the house like that.

You're overreacting. Now come back here and get your note. I may not agree with you one hundred percent, but I'll give you permission to help out at Dr. Fayette's office. And to bring home the dog."

I stopped and slowly turned around. There Dad stood, holding open the screen door. My piece of paper fluttered from his fingertips.

6
Gumption

By the end of the second week, Champ was ready to come home. I could tell he was feeling better. As soon as I walked into the back room of Dr. Fayette's office, I heard his tail beating against the stainless-steel cage. He couldn't wait for me to set him on the floor. Then he'd hop-step behind me, watching when I scooped out the cats' litter boxes and scrubbed out the rest of the cages.

"Dogs are like that," Dr. Fayette told me. "They don't focus on their shortcomings at all. They adapt. We could learn a lot from them."

I had already learned plenty. I learned how to look at the place where Champ's leg used to be without letting my stomach lurch up to my throat.

I'd also learned that Champ grunted when I scratched his left ear and that he put his nose in my hand when he wanted me to pet him. Which was all the time.

Thanks to Dr. Fayette, I also knew how to brush Champ's black-and-white coat until it shone. I liked the way a blaze of white reached up from his black nose to meet the black between his ears. I also found out that border collies are smart. They are so smart they could understand hand signals and whistles when herding sheep. Of course, Champ probably had never even seen sheep, since he'd spent his entire life living in Mrs. Lerner's kennels. Another thing I figured out without Dr. Fayette's help: Border collies also like to stare, and Champ was no exception. He would lock his brown eyes on me as I did my work and watch the entire time.

"Thank you, Riley," Dr. Fayette said as Champ and I got ready to leave. "You did good work here at the office."

"Thanks for helping me out, Dr. Fayette," I

said as we got ready to leave. "But now that I have to go straight home from school to take Champ out, I don't know how I'll be able to keep working."

"You're welcome anytime, Riley, but you've done enough already," he said. He gave Champ a final scratch between the ears. "You two are going to get along just great. I have to admit, I had a few doubts at first, but not anymore. This was the perfect solution."

Of course, Dr. Fayette didn't know my dad very well. If he had, he would have had plenty of doubts. Dad hadn't mentioned Champ since handing me the note saying it would be okay for me to bring the dog home, but he had noticed that I wasn't practicing for the baseball team anymore. How could I practice when I was working so hard at Dr. Fayette's office? I knew Dad thought I was quitting the baseball team before I even started, which wasn't so. I had just put it on hold for a while.

Mom took off work early and stopped the car in front of Dr. Fayette's office. She set her mouth in a tight line when Champ and I came out the door. Champ hop-stepped next to me as if he'd had three legs his entire life. Still, Mom drove slow, taking the corners at a snail's speed. Champ hopped back and forth across the backseat, whining as he looked out the window.

"He must be scared to be riding in a car," Mom said, glancing in the rearview mirror. She didn't finish her thought. I did.

"Guess you can't blame him," I said. "The last time he was in a car he had four legs. Now look at him."

"He looks fine, Riley," Mom said in a firm voice. "His chest is so white."

Of course, Mr. Douglas was in his garden when Mom pulled into the driveway. He stood up, a weed dangling dirty roots from his fingers. He watched Mom park in the shade of the garage.

I barely had the car door open when Kaylee pedaled down the driveway on her bike. "Where is he?" she hollered as she hopped off her bike and let it drop to the grass.

It's hard to ignore people when they're staring

at you, but that's what I tried to do when I lifted Champ down from the backseat of Mom's car. I sat him on the driveway. Gently. Champ tried to take one step, then sat down. He looked from Kaylee to Mom and back to me.

Kaylee reached out and rubbed Champ's forehead. "I think he's great. Just because he limps, it doesn't mean a thing."

"Nothing wrong with a limp," Mr. Douglas said as he leaned on the fence that separated our yards. "If there was, I'd be about the most useless thing around." Mom laughed along with Mr. Douglas.

I had to admit, Champ looked good. His black-and-white fur was smooth from the brushing I'd given him. His eyes were bright and his tail swept loose gravel from the driveway. Maybe Kaylee was right.

Everything was going to be great. Just great.

When Dad got home from work he eyed Champ as if he were a flattened football. "Are you sure you know what you're getting into?" he asked me.

I kneeled down and scratched Champ's chin. I

couldn't help but smile just a little when Champ licked my cheek. "You don't have to worry. I'll take care of him all by myself. You won't have to do a thing."

"Riley learned a lot working for Dr. Fayette," Mom said, giving Dad a quick hug as she walked by. "I think he knows what it takes to keep a dog."

I didn't think Dad believed a word. I could tell by the way one of his eyebrows arched up into his forehead. I was the one, after all, who had given up on three sports and had recently smashed a toothpick bridge to smithereens. My record for completing projects wasn't exactly stellar. Dad probably considered Champ another failed project.

I figured, being handicapped and all, Champ would stay on the back porch and pretty much lie there. That night, I made a nest for him out of an old blanket and filled one bowl with water and another with dried food. Champ watched the entire time. I lifted him up and sat him down in the middle of the blanket. "There you go," I told him, like that settled everything. It didn't. As soon as I turned to go inside, Champ stood up, balancing perfectly fine on his three legs, and hop-stepped after me.

"Get back on your bed," I told him, gently shoving him to the corner, but he wouldn't have anything to do with the blanket. He followed me all the way across the porch and stood by the back door when I went inside. That wasn't the worst part. I'd only made it to the top of the stairs when he started barking. I'm not talking a yip here and there. I'm talking full-fledged *bark-bark-bark*. The kind that only stopped for him to snuffle air and then get started again.

"Riley!" Mom hollered. "Your dog's barking."

Like I didn't already know.

It didn't matter what I told Champ, every time I closed the door he barked. For a big-time championship show dog, he didn't seem too smart to me. He didn't understand "hush" or "quiet" or even "shut up."

"Champ's barking," Kaylee said the next day. She had come over first thing in the morning so we could walk to school together.

Why do people insist on saying the obvious? Everybody on our block knew Champ was barking.

I was running late, still eating breakfast when she got there. That's because I had to keep going to the back door to make Champ quiet down.

"Hurry up," Kaylee said. "We're going to be late."

"Your dog is going to have the neighbors calling us," Dad said. "You had better do something about that noise this afternoon."

"I'm trying," I told Dad.

"You'll just have to try harder," Dad said, with a rattle of the newspaper.

I glared at him for a full five seconds, then grabbed my book bag. I let the door slam when Kaylee and I stepped out to the porch, even though I knew that was one thing my mom couldn't stand.

As soon as I got on the porch, Champ stopped his barking and snuffled my hand. "Dumb dog," I said.

"I think he's pretty smart," Kaylee said. "He trained you to open the door when he barks."

Kaylee was the second person I glared at that morning. Champ didn't seem a bit bothered that he was causing so much trouble. In fact, his tail swept through the air so fast, it whipped Kaylee on the knee. "He already loves you," Kaylee said. "You sure are lucky to have a dog."

I smiled. She was absolutely right about that. I looked straight into Champ's eyes and held his head still. "Stop barking," I warned. "Or Mr. Douglas will come after you with his pruning shears."

When we left the porch, Champ watched us until we rounded the corner of the house. He was standing in the exact same place when I got home, as if he hadn't moved a hair.

Every day was the same. It was as if Champ stood there the whole time, waiting for me to come around the corner of the house. After I'd had him for a week, I found out that wasn't exactly true.

One afternoon after school, Kaylee was perched on her bike, waiting for me to get my glove for a practice session at the empty lot. She still hadn't given up on me as a baseball player. Kaylee doesn't give up on anything. She said she was persistent. I called her stubborn.

She was trying to ignore Mr. Douglas, who was pretending to pull weeds from around his forsythia bush, but we both knew he was spying. As soon as I hopped down the porch steps, Champ started barking. Mr. Douglas stood up, rubbed his back, and nodded in our direction.

"Sounds like that dog of yours is ready to get off the porch," Mr. Douglas called before I could hop on my bike and speed away.

In a situation like this, kids have two choices. They can pretend they didn't hear a word and go on about their business or they can stop and answer the adult. To ignore the comment would mean you have to go on about your business without a hint that you heard. I wasn't quick enough. When Mr. Douglas spoke, I made the mistake of looking in his direction. It was too late to ignore him. Kaylee, on the other hand, made no mistakes. She pedaled down the driveway and turned down the street as if she hadn't heard a thing.

I sighed and leaned the bike against my hip.

"He gets off the porch," I explained. "Three times a day I take him to the yard so he can, um, you know, do his business."

That was something else I had learned about dogs that was way different from hamsters and fish. They made bigger messes that were not the least bit pleasant to clean up. I did clean them up, though. I knew that if Dad stepped in a stinking pile in the backyard, I'd never hear the end of it.

Mr. Douglas nodded. "Been noticing how he likes getting out in that yard. Likes having you around. Likes having you around so much, he barks just about all day long until you get home."

Finally he was getting around to saying what he really meant.

"Sorry if he bothers you," I told Mr. Douglas. "I've been trying to get him to be quiet." I'd been telling Mom and Dad the same thing every day, too.

Mr. Douglas smiled as if he was being friendly, but I knew better. He was being a busybody of a neighbor. "Border collies are bred to work. They need a job to do or they get bored. Maybe if you took him with you, he'd get so worn out he wouldn't bark as much," Mr. Douglas suggested.

"He'd never make it to the ball lot," I said, and I must admit I let my eyes roll. I figured he wouldn't see. After all, he hadn't noticed a big thing like a missing leg.

"He might surprise you," Mr. Douglas said. "He just might surprise you at that."

And then Mr. Douglas turned away as if he'd just told me the answers to all of next year's math tests. I rode away, trying to ignore Champ's bark-bark-barking, which was pretty hard to do until I got at least two blocks away. I didn't realize a dog's bark could reach so far.

Neighbors started calling the following week, confirming that Champ's barking was getting on more than just my dad's nerves, which I knew since Dad made it a point to tell me every night that I had to do something about the noise. On Wednesday, Mom came in from work and told me to have a seat in the dining room. I knew then and there that this was not going to be a hi-how-have-you-been-doing kind of talk. This was a you're-going-to-sit-there-and-listen-to-what's-good-for-you lecture.

Mom kicked off her good shoes and fell back in the chair. She rubbed the toes on her right foot and sighed. "Something has to be done about that dog, Riley," she said. "He spends the entire day on the porch barking. If you can't get him to stop, then the neighbors are going to end up tarring and feathering your father. I'm sure you don't want that to happen."

I swallowed and nodded but I didn't say anything. I couldn't think of anything to say. Besides, Champ was busy barking. That didn't help matters.

"This afternoon your dad was working on the air conditioner for Mr. McIntyre in the next block. He told your dad he was tired of listening to Champ barking. And that's not the first complaint he's had."

It surprised me that Dad hadn't told me he'd gotten complaints from the neighbors, but I didn't have a chance to ask about them because Mom kept talking.

"You have to do something, Riley, or your

father is going to cart that dog off to the pound," Mom said.

I suddenly felt like I had swallowed a baseball. "He can't do that," I said. "It's not Champ's fault that he can't do anything besides sit on the porch."

Mom sighed and started rubbing the toes on her left foot. "Of course he can do more than that," she said. "It's not fair to keep Champ on the porch all the time. Why not take him for a walk or something?"

"He's crippled, Mom," I said, speaking slowly to make sure she caught every word.

"Well," Mom said, with an eye roll of her own, "you can't let him sit out there, day in and day out, disturbing the neighbors. Besides, that dog can walk just fine."

"I bet he'd be happier inside during the day," I said. "That way if he barks, nobody could hear him."

Mom didn't look convinced.

"He's housetrained," I said in a rush, "so you wouldn't have to worry about him messing on the rugs. And that way he won't bother the neighbors. Can't we try it? Please?"

Mom sighed. "We'll try it on one condition," she said. "You get up in the morning and take him for a walk and you come straight home after school for another walk."

"But . . ."

"No buts, Riley," Mom said. "He can stay in the house during the day, but you have to walk him in the morning and afternoon. And he'd better not ruin my carpets!"

I knew I better quit while I was ahead. "Thanks, Mom," I said. I smiled so wide it hurt my cheeks and said the words I knew melted my mom every time. "You're the greatest."

I bolted from the dining room and threw open the door to the porch. Champ's tail-wagging took over for the barking when he saw me. I was beginning to like the way he looked right up at my face and started wiggling all over whenever I showed up. I held open the door and Champ hopped in as if he owned the place. "See," I told Mom. "He's not going to bother a thing."

That night Champ followed me upstairs to my bed. I got ready to hoist him up and carry him, but he put his only front paw on the step and then hopped up by himself, step-by-step.

I wasn't the only one impressed. Mom looped her arm around Dad's waist as they both watched Champ climb the stairs. "You have to admit," Mom said, "that dog doesn't let anything stop him. He's got what you call gumption."

Dad wasn't about to admit anything, but I did notice he stood at the bottom of the steps and watched Champ make his way to the very top.

It was nice drifting off to sleep, knowing Champ was on the floor where my hand could dangle over the edge to touch his ear. " 'Night, Champ," I mumbled.

I heard his tail sweep across the floor at the sound of his name.

7
Triple-header Day

Over the next three weeks, my days got longer and longer. Sometimes, when the alarm clock woke me, I'd slap it off and turn over. But there was no way Champ would let me get back to sleep. He'd snuffle at the covers, find my pajamas, and tug until I'd slide out of bed. Mom was right. Champ liked going for morning walks. He'd sniff every bush and tree to the corner and back.

After school, I had to hurry home to walk him around the yard and play tug-of-war with his chew toy. Two afternoons a week I'd head for Dr. Fayette's office. The other days I'd go to ball practice. I thought it would be hard going back to practice and facing the gang after I had stormed off the field, but the only one who seemed to remember was Erica. Besides, I couldn't quit. If I did, I knew Dad would think I was a failure. Again.

Sign-ups for the Davenport Summer League were just two weeks away and I still couldn't hit the ball to save my life. Erica had reminded me at least thirteen times to be on time for practice so I needed to hurry, but I knew there was no way I would make it in time that afternoon. As soon as I stepped inside the house I knew there would be trouble.

"What have you done?" I yelped. Champ's only answer was his nose pushing against my leg, guiding me to the door.

I took a deep breath, dropped my backpack, and pushed Champ away. "Bad dog," I said.

Champ wagged his tail. I swore he was grinning.

"What did he do?" Kaylee asked, shoving her way past me.

Pillows and bedspreads were piled in the middle of the kitchen. "Bad dog," I said again. I scooped up the linens and headed upstairs. Sure enough, all the beds were stripped bare. I looked down at Champ, wondering at the strength it took to tug every spread, blanket, sheet, and pillow down the steps. "Didn't you get tired?" I asked him. "Didn't the place where your leg used to be hurt?"

Champ wagged his tail and woofed, ready to play. He nudged his nose into my hand, waiting for a head scratch, but I didn't feel like scratching his ears.

"Champ's obviously been busy," Kaylee said when she peeked in the dining room. Piled in the center of the floor were shoes. Not just one or two shoes, but a mountain of shoes. Even I could tell a few of them had suspicious teeth marks. Champ cocked his head and lifted an ear, looking pleased with himself.

"I am in so much trouble," I said.

Kaylee bent down to look at the pile of shoes. "Champ must've spent half the day fetching every shoe in the house." She held up one of Mom's new sneakers. "And it looks like he spent the other half chewing holes in them."

"You have to help me put these away," I said,

dumping my book bag on the counter and kneeling down. I scooped up a handful of shoes. Champ immediately grabbed my shirt collar with his teeth and hung on tight. I fell to the floor, shoes scattering under the chairs.

I pushed Champ aside to scoop up shoes and hurried upstairs. Champ followed me every step of the way, snapping at shoestrings, thinking this was a big game of keep-away.

Kaylee and I were on our third trip up the stairs when Dad walked in. Usually, he has to work late into the evening on broken fans and leaking air conditioners. Sometimes, when he's in the neighborhood, he stops by the house for a few minutes. Today was one of those days.

I heard the back door close and looked down at Champ. He looked up at me with a wide dog-smile. He didn't seem to understand the seriousness of the situation. Even if he did have a big-time pedigree and blue ribbons decorating Mrs. Lerner's walls, sometimes I thought Champ didn't have any smarts at all.

"Riley!" Dad yelled.

I dumped a pile of shoes on my bed and took a deep breath. "Time to face the music," I said.

"Not me," Kaylee said. "I'm not in the mood for music!"

Kaylee mumbled a hello to my dad, mouthed, 'good luck' to me, then slipped out the back door.

Dad stood in the middle of the kitchen, holding his loafer. "Did your dog do this?" he asked.

My dad could ask the stupidest questions. I nodded. What else could I do?

"You've got to get that dog under control," Dad said. "What do you plan to do about him?"

"I'm putting the shoes away," I said, and I didn't say it all that nicely. "If we keep our closets closed, it won't happen again. I'll remake the beds when I get home from practice."

"This has nothing to do with us keeping our closets closed, Riley," Dad said, his voice getting louder and louder, like a windup toy about to take off. "This is about you and your dog. You wanted Champ, but you haven't done a thing to train him. He's taking over this house, and now he's chewed a hole in my dress shoes. Having a dog isn't something you can take lightly. It's not something you sign up for and then quit two days later."

There it was. The real reason Dad was yelling.

"I'm not quitting," I told him. "I'm still trying out for the team."

"I'm glad to hear it," Dad said. "I know it's been hard juggling school, practice, and a new pet. But you're going to have to face the fact that Champ needs more of your attention."

I wasn't about to admit it out loud, but Dad had a point. "I'll take care of him," I told him. I grabbed Champ's collar and led him out the back door.

Champ nudged my leg, pushing me over to the picnic table, his nose a gentle pressure on my leg.

"Border collies do that," Mr. Douglas called across the fence. "They're herders."

I hadn't seen Mr. Douglas at first because he was sitting in the swing under the big tree in his yard. With spring in full force, the leaves had filled out and cast a huge shadow across the lawn. Spirals of wood shavings littered the ground around his feet from the piece of wood he was whittling. A few more fell from his lap when he stood up. Mr. Douglas held his back and slowly straightened up before walking through the gate that separates our yards. The bench creaked when Mr. Douglas settled down next to me.

I ran my fingers through Champ's hair. He leaned against my leg and grunted. "I guess you're right," I told Mr. Douglas. "Champ spent the day herding every shoe in our house to the dining room. Then he decided to unmake the beds and drag the sheets to the kitchen."

Mr. Douglas's eyes were lost in wrinkles when he laughed. For the life of me, I couldn't figure out what he thought was so funny. I glanced up at the kitchen window. Dad was standing at the sink, looking out. If Mr. Douglas noticed, he didn't say anything.

Mr. Douglas's face was tanned by the long hours he spent gardening. His brown skin stood out against his silver hair. "You're doing a good job with that dog," Mr. Douglas said.

Normally I wouldn't say two words to Mr. Douglas unless I had to, but I wanted the whole world to know how unfair my dad was and figured I could start with Mr. Douglas. "Not according to Dad," I said. "He thinks it's my fault that Champ barks and chews stuff."

Champ put his chin on my knees and looked into my eyes. It was the look of total trust. It was the same look he'd given Mrs. Lerner right before she had condemned him to death.

Mr. Douglas reached down and scratched one of Champ's ears. "I know a little about dogs. Had a few in my younger days."

Great. First Champ decided to use shoes as chew toys. Then Dad came home from work early. Now the crazy man next door was going to tell me what I was doing wrong. It was turning out to be a triple-header of a day.

"Border collies are an active breed," Mr. Douglas said. "Smart, too. I imagine a smart dog like Champ gets pretty bored sitting around day in and day out. Especially since he's used to getting a lot of attention training for those fancy dog shows."

"Bored?" I repeated with a little snort of a laugh. "Dogs don't get bored."

"Sure they do," Mr. Douglas said. "I've been bored ever since they made me retire. Wasn't so bad when my wife was here to keep me company. But now that I'm on my own, I've learned the meaning of boredom very well, and I recognize boredom when I see it."

I had never thought about Mr. Douglas being bored. "I figured you had plenty to do, snipping flowers and whittling wood," I blurted.

Mr. Douglas laughed. Not a polite grown-up laugh, but a laugh from deep in his belly that made his head tilt back. "It keeps my hands busy," he said. "Keeps me from going nuts. I'm thinking that's exactly how your dog's feeling. He's used to competing. Maybe he'd like to compete again."

I scratched Champ's left ear and shook my head. "His competing days are long gone. Thanks to . . ." I almost said it. I almost took the blame and said "thanks to me," but I stopped myself just in time. If Mr. Douglas noticed, he didn't show it.

"Maybe he can't do those highfalutin competitions where the ladies dress in high heels and run around the ring with their pooches," Mr. Douglas said with a shake of his head. "Never could figure out why they dress like that to go out and play with their dogs. Seems like blue jeans and sneakers would be better. I understand a dog has to be perfect to be in the contests that this dog used to win."

"Exactly," I said. "And Champ isn't perfect. Not anymore."

"Well, maybe he can't be in that kind of competition, but I bet he could do one of those other kind that's just for fun."

Even though I knew it was pointless, I couldn't help but ask. "What kind is that?"

"That kind they started having at the Founders Day Celebration," Mr. Douglas explained. "Read about it last year in the newspaper. The way I remember it, the dogs and kids work as a team to run an obstacle course."

Every June, the leaders of Davenport held a picnic to celebrate the founding of our town. There were barbecues, watermelon-eating contests, and horseshoe games. It was also when the Summer League teams kick off their season.

As soon as Mr. Douglas said "obstacle course" I knew exactly what he meant. I'd watched the event last year between eating hot dogs and playing tug-of-war. I shook my head before Mr. Douglas wasted any more of his breath. "Forget it," I said. "A three-legged dog and a sports-challenged kid have no hope of winning something that involves jumping over bars and getting past obstacles."

Mr. Douglas let loose with another one of those belly laughs, though I didn't see a darn thing funny about what I said.

"It has nothing to do with winning, Riley," Mr. Douglas said. "Nothing at all."

8
A Different Kind of Show

Mr. Douglas was puttering around in his garage when I climbed on my bike to leave, and I wondered for an instant what he was doing before I pedaled down the driveway.

A bunch of kids were getting in one last practice at the empty lot before signing up on Saturday for the official team. As soon as Kaylee saw me, she jogged over to see what happened between Dad and me. Then I told her everything Mr. Douglas had said.

We sat on the grass under a maple tree, watching Erica pitch a fastball to Luke. I didn't believe anybody could hit one of Erica's fastballs, but Luke did. His bat smacked the ball and sent it sailing high toward second base. Erica waited until Luke was safe on first base before she looked my way.

"See, Riley?" Erica said. "That's the way it's done. Now you try."

"Not now," I told her. "I'm busy."

Erica gave me her best I-want-to-beat-you-up look. "You'll never help the team if you don't show up to practice on time. You have to at least try," she told me before turning and heading back to the pitcher's mound. I stuck out my tongue, but she didn't see it since her back was to me.

"So are you going to do it?" Kaylee asked.

"Do what?" I asked.

"Enter Champ in the contest?"

"Of course not," I said. "It's a stupid idea."

"What's so stupid about it?" Kaylee asked. "I think it's a great idea. Just think what old Mrs. Lerner would say if Champ won a blue ribbon. And what about your dad! He wouldn't know what to do if you came home carrying a ribbon."

For a split second I imagined the feel of a blue ribbon in my hands. The look on Dad's face when

I presented it to him. The pat on my back he'd surely give me. But the bubble popped as soon as Champ limped into my daydream. "It would only give my dad another chance to see me lose," I said. "There's no way a three-legged dog could win one of those contests. They probably wouldn't even let me enter Champ."

"You don't know that," Kaylee said. "I'll help you find out more about it."

That's why we headed to the library after I struck out three times during baseball practice.

Usually, Kaylee and I only went to the library during the summer when the days stretched out long and hot. Chuck the librarian grinned at us when we walked through the double doors. "Look what the cat dragged in," he said. "You must have a huge assignment at school."

Kaylee smiled right back at Chuck. "Nope," she said. "We're here to learn something all on our own."

"Will wonders never cease?" Chuck asked. I was sure his laugh echoed all the way back to the mystery section. I waited for another librarian to shush him but nobody did. I guess librarians are allowed to be louder than kids.

"Riley needs to find out about dog shows," Kaylee said. She was talking as loud as Chuck, and I felt my ears redden. I looked around to see if anyone was staring.

"Dog shows," Chuck said, suddenly serious as he typed in a few words on his computer. "We have lots of titles. Let me show you the section and see if you can find something that fits the bill."

We followed Chuck to the shelves in the middle of the library. Once there, he left us to look at book after book. Most of them were old, showing black-and-white pictures of men and women dressed in outfits from the 60s and 70s. "They look downright silly running around in dresses and suits, if you ask me," Kaylee said, sounding just like Mr. Douglas.

I had to agree. I tried to imagine Mrs. Lerner dressed up, trotting next to Champ. I paged through one of the books. "Dr. Fayette was right,"

I whispered to Kaylee. "This says each breed has to meet certain standards."

"What's a standard?" Kaylee asked, without even looking up from her book.

"Depends on the dog," I told her. "Some have to have a specific color of nose or eyes. Others have to have a coat that's straight and doesn't curl. Or their tail has to be carried just so. If they don't meet the standards, they don't stand a chance."

"That's not fair," Kaylee said. "A dog can't help the way he's born."

I knew about fair and unfair. I also knew about not meeting someone else's standards. "No," I said. "It's not fair. And I'm pretty sure having three legs wouldn't fit the standard for any dog."

"Mr. Douglas said there was a kind of show where that wouldn't matter," Kaylee reminded me.

I didn't say anything. I was still looking at the requirements for some of the dog breeds. The judges were totally unforgiving if a dog had a fault. Unforgiving. Like my dad. It was so unfair.

"This is pointless," I said. I slammed the book

shut and stuffed it back onto the shelf. Then I grabbed another book. A newer one that at least had colored pictures. I flipped through the pages in a hurry, ready to leave the library and the whole idea of a dog show for Champ, until something near the end of the book caught my eye. Pictures different from the others. These pictures showed dogs jumping over bars, running through tunnels, balancing on planks of wood poised high above the ground. Owners were in motion beside them, and these people weren't wearing suits and ties. They had on shorts and sneakers and all of them were laughing. It looked like a day at an amusement park for dogs.

"That's it," Kaylee said, looking over my shoulder. "That's the thing Mr. Douglas was talking about. What's it say?"

I turned to the first page of the chapter. "It's called agility," I told her. "During agility trials, dogs complete a timed run through a course that includes weaving around poles, hopping through tires, jumping over bars, balancing across a teeter-totter, running through tunnels, and navigating across a bridge."

"Looks like fun," Kaylee said. "Champ would love it. At least check out the book and see what it's all about."

I took the book to the counter and waited while Chuck waved the wand over the bar code. He turned the book over, glancing at the title. "Thinking about entering a dog show?" he asked. "What kind of dog do you have?"

"Border collie," I mumbled. "But I'm not going to be in a show. Just curious about agility contests, that's all."

Chuck clapped his hands, making me jump. "Agility. That's a totally awesome event. It's like a doggy day at the park. I went to the one last year. Had a blast. Dogs love it. Any kind of dog can participate. I have a mutt from the pound, and I thought about getting him involved, too. You should give it a try."

I slipped the book off the counter and nodded. "I'll think about it," I told him. "Thanks."

When Kaylee and I got back to my house, she plopped down on the picnic table bench to catch her breath. Not me. I heard Champ barking from the kitchen. I let him outside, nearly tripping when he bumped against my legs. I couldn't help but laugh as he pushed me farther and farther from the house.

"That dog's going to herd you clear to Arkansas," Mr. Douglas said. He stood in the shadows of his garage, but now he stepped out into the sun and crossed the narrow strip of grass that separates our two driveways. Champ didn't realize he wasn't supposed to be friendly with Mr. Douglas. My dog went right to him and looked up, waiting for Mr. Douglas to give him a head rub. Mr. Douglas did exactly that.

"See you got a book on dog shows," Mr. Douglas said, with a nod to the book lying on the picnic table. He didn't miss a thing.

"Riley's finding out about agility courses," Kaylee said.

Mr. Douglas walked the rest of the way to the picnic table as if he'd been invited to dinner.

"Yep," Mr. Douglas said, flipping to the chapter on agility courses. "That's what I was talking about. The obstacle course is built to appeal to dogs. Looks like the bridge and teeter-totter are the hardest, slows them down and takes concentration. A dog and his owner would have to spend a lot of time practicing. I imagine that's the part dogs like the best, though." I glanced at the pictures. Both obstacles had yellow bases that dogs had to touch going up and down. The teeter-totter was the worst since the dogs had to pause in the middle and wait for the board to shift like a teeter-totter.

"Champ couldn't compete against other dogs," I said. "It's a timed competition. He couldn't beat dogs with all their legs."

Mr. Douglas slapped me on the back so hard I had to grab the bench to keep from falling over. "Coming in last isn't what makes you a loser," he said. "Not winning is just not coming in first. Not trying is the mark of a real loser. Now, I have a feeling Champ doesn't care if he comes in first, second, or nine-hundred-and-ninety-ninth. It wouldn't hurt to at least give it a try. We could set up a few obstacles in the yard. See what Champ can do."

I shrugged, since it didn't really matter, anyway. "Can't. I don't have the kind of obstacles they talk about in this book," I said as if that was the final word.

It wasn't. Mr. Douglas turned and walked back toward his garage. "Well, then," he called over his shoulder, "I guess we'd better get busy!"

9
Half the Battle

I heard the saw as soon as I got home from school the next day. I didn't have time to think about what Mr. Douglas might be doing in his garage. I had to let Champ out before I headed to ball practice. Champ took his sweet time sniffing every fence post and bush. He snuffled a leaf and moseyed to the next fence post. Then his ears lifted nearly an inch and he pointed his nose toward the sounds coming from Mr. Douglas's garage. I looked at my watch. I was already late. Erica was really going to let me have it.

I realized it was suddenly quiet and looked next door. Mr. Douglas stood there, wiping his hands on a dirty cloth. His silver hair tumbled down over a forehead shining with sweat. The sun reflected off his glasses so I couldn't see his eyes, but I knew where he was looking. He was watching me, of course.

"Been puttering around the garage," he said. "Come see what you think when Champ gets finished doing his business."

I was already late for practice, so I figured I might as well check out what Mr. Douglas was doing. As soon as I had cleaned up Champ's business and dumped it in the garbage, I snapped my fingers for Champ's attention. We walked through the gate and across the narrow strip of grass that separated our yards.

Mr. Douglas's garage was like any other on our street. Since we live in a neighborhood as old as dirt, the garages aren't part of the houses. They sit in the backyard like giant outhouses. The siding on Mr. Douglas's garage was once painted white, but now the paint is chipping off in huge flakes and the whole structure leans to the left. Once, not too long ago, I had pushed against the side of his garage that faced our backyard, to see if I could make the whole thing fall to the ground. It was a lot sturdier than it looked.

I hesitated inside the open door, letting my eyes adjust to the dim light. I heard Champ's nails clicking across the flaking cement, straight toward the back of the garage where Mr. Douglas waited for us.

It was at least twenty degrees cooler in the garage. Dust tickled my nose and it smelled like a mixture of rubber, oil, and dirt. A mountain of boxes crowded the right side of the double garage, leaving room for a dark green Buick that was so old it might be considered a classic. A tube of light flickered above a window in the back wall, and an open side door let in a narrow stream of sun.

"I'm back here," Mr. Douglas said, reaching his hand down to meet Champ's head. I made my way between the boxes and car to where Mr. Douglas stood.

"How do you like it?" Mr. Douglas asked.

An old plastic garbage can with the bottom cut out was lying on its side on his workbench. "What is it?" I asked.

"A tunnel," he said as he lifted the barrel and put it on the floor. "According to that library book, it's a favorite for dogs. Thought you might want to start out with that one and see how Champ does."

I looked at the homemade tunnel. Champ was sniffing the edge as if he might pee on it. "I don't think Champ would know what to do," I said.

"Not unless you show him," Mr. Douglas said. "That's part of the fun. How about you two giving it a try?"

I thought about the rest of the kids practicing at the empty field, but considering the way I had struck out the day before, I figured the team wouldn't care if I was late or not. Besides, it would only take a few minutes to prove Mr. Douglas had wasted his afternoon.

"Fine," I said. "Let's get it over with."

"That's the spirit," Mr. Douglas said as he scooped up the barrel and hugged it to his chest. "Trying is half the battle."

I followed him outside. Champ followed Mr. Douglas, looking up at the barrel as if it were a new game. Which, I guess, it was. When Mr. Douglas set the barrel down on the ground Champ sniffed at it, then looked at me.

"See?" I said. "He doesn't have a clue."

"Then show him," Mr. Douglas suggested.

"What do you mean?" I asked. "There's nothing wrong with his eyes. He can see it there in front of his nose."

Mr. Douglas laughed, his eyes almost disappearing in wrinkles. "I mean get down on your knees and show him how it's done."

"You want me to go through that thing?" I asked. I could just imagine what Erica would say if she saw me crawling on my hands and knees while my dog sat and watched. I'd never hear the end of it.

"I'd do it myself," Mr. Douglas said, "but my knees are shot."

I knew I could spend the rest of the day arguing, or I could drop to the ground and get it over with. As soon as I hit the ground, Champ covered my face with licks. I pushed him aside and crawled into the barrel.

Champ peered inside and woofed.

"See?" I said. "He doesn't get it."

The words were barely out of my mouth when Champ scrambled inside with me. "That's the way," Mr. Douglas yelled. "Now scoot out the other side."

When we got to the other end, Champ jumped up, placing his one front paw on my shoulder. His tail wagged and he licked my chin. "You did it," I said. "You really did it. Good boy!" I couldn't help feeling a little proud of my dog.

Mr. Douglas slapped his thighs. "Now, we just have to convince him to do it when you tell him to," he said. "You think that dog's smart enough for that?"

"Of course he's smart," I said without thinking. After all, this was the dog that had figured out how to unmake every bed in our house.

Climbing through a barrel turned out to be something a three-legged dog definitely could do. Getting him to do it when I told him was another matter altogether. Mr. Douglas sat in the old swing and watched. When I pointed at the barrel, Champ jumped for my finger. When I got down and pretended I was going to go through on my hands and knees again, Champ tried to tackle me from behind. When I tried throwing a stick through the tunnel, Champ hopped around to the other side and brought the stick back dangling from his mouth, without setting a single paw inside the obstacle. I had just figured out that throwing a treat inside the barrel was a surefire way of getting Champ to go through the tunnel on his own when Kaylee rode her bike up the driveway.

"Where have you been?" she asked, stopping just shy of Mr. Douglas's property line. Her baseball mitt dangled from the handlebars.

"I forgot about practice," I said honestly. "But look what Champ can do." I tossed a doggy treat. "Tunnel," I said in a serious voice.

Champ scurried through the barrel and waited for me to scratch his ears once he got to the other side.

Kaylee propped her bike against the side of my garage and leaned against the fence separating Mr. Douglas's yard from mine. "You taught him that in one afternoon?"

I grinned. "He's a fast learner," I bragged.

"Does this mean you're going to enter the contest on Founders Day, after all?" she asked.

"I didn't say I was entering a contest," I told her. "I just wanted to see if Champ could do it, that's all. I wonder what else he can do."

Of course, the only way to find out was to build more obstacles, which is exactly what Mr. Douglas did. Each day, he waited for me after school. So did Champ.

Mr. Douglas, it turned out, knew quite a bit about woodworking. "When I was younger," he told me, "I built tables and bookshelves and even that old swing for my wife. Making these obstacles shouldn't be a problem. No problem at all."

All I had to do was mention an idea for a new obstacle and Mr. Douglas would nod as he thought it through. He taught me how to pound in nails without splitting the wood. He showed me how to use a saw and the sander. I learned to use a level, brackets, nuts, and bolts. He taught me how to fashion a balance beam and teeter-totter out of wood planks and sawhorses. He made jumping bars using plastic pipes, and it was my idea to use a folded lounge chair as a pause table.

I liked making useful things out of old junk. Working on the obstacles reminded me of building toothpick bridges. Taking scraps of lumber, rope, and old pipes and putting them together until they formed something totally different was a challenge. Only this was better than the toothpick bridge, because everything we built was actually being used by Champ.

And Champ loved it all.

Dad came home early from work and watched us one day, leaning on the fence. He nodded to Mr. Douglas. "Pretty impressive," he said. "You've been putting a lot of work into that doggy playground," he said.

"Your son has a way with tools," Mr. Douglas said.

It hit me that nobody had ever said I was good at anything before. It felt nice to know Mr. Douglas thought I had a talent for building things.

I wanted Dad to see how Champ knew to scramble through the trash-can tunnel and then head for the jumping bars that I'd help build. "Watch this," I said.

But Dad turned to face Mr. Douglas, so he didn't see Champ hop over the bars and make his way to the teeter-totter. "I appreciate you spending so much time with my boy. Sorry about the clutter in your yard. I could help you move it over here."

"I don't mind at all," Mr. Douglas said while I coaxed Champ up one side of the teeter-totter.

Unfortunately, Dad glanced over at me just as Champ backed away. "Let me know when you get tired of it and I'll help you take it down," Dad told Mr. Douglas before he turned and disappeared inside the house.

The next week, Mr. Douglas found a tire in his garage that he thought we could use for the tire jump. We just needed something to hang it from. When he started pulling down the old swing Mrs. Douglas had once used, I stopped him. "Are you sure you want to use this frame for Champ?" I asked. Mom had told me it was Mrs. Douglas's favorite spot to sit.

Mr. Douglas nodded. "My wife, Helen, would be

proud to have you use it," he said. Then he unhooked the swing and hung the tire from the cross pole, making sure the tire dangled close to the ground. He anchored it with ropes to the four legs of the frame, so the tire wouldn't swing out of control.

After we finished making each obstacle, we spent a few days letting Champ get used to them. Some of them, like the tunnel, he could do in a snap. As long as the jump bars and tire were hung low enough, he didn't seem to have trouble hopping over them, either. The teeter-totter and balance beam were another matter. They required balance. Something any three-legged dog would have trouble with.

After nearly two weeks, Champ still didn't like the feel of the wooden plank that led him up to the balance beam. I coaxed him, held out my hands to give him support. Still, he didn't want to try. The same with the teeter-totter. Champ bypassed those to hop up on the folded lounge chair.

The pause table was no problem for him since Mrs. Lerner had trained him well for conformation and obedience trials. He knew the commands "down" and "stay." "Good boy," I told him. Champ would wag his tail so hard, his entire body wiggled at the words.

"He's coming along," Mr. Douglas said. "I think he'll be ready for that competition at the picnic."

I hugged Champ. Since we'd been practicing, he'd grown stronger. He didn't bark as much and nothing in the house had been herded to the middle of the kitchen, either. It was true he could do most of the obstacles, but I still knew he couldn't win a contest. Not a contest based on speed and agility.

"I'm not entering the contest," I told Mr. Douglas for the bazillionth time. "Champ is doing great, but he can't win."

"Winning doesn't always mean coming in first," Mr. Douglas said.

I thought Mr. Douglas was certifiably nuts but knew enough not to say it out loud. I didn't have to. Dad said it for me.

10
King of Cool

With all that building and practicing going on, I totally forgot to sign up for the Summer League team. Well, to be honest, I didn't forget. I knew exactly when sign-ups were since Kaylee talked about baseball morning, noon, and night. I didn't want to give Dad another reason to call me a quitter, but I had been too busy.

"How can you stand to spend so much time with him?" Kaylee whispered to me one afternoon. She still stopped by before baseball practice, just to see if I could make it.

I knew who she was talking about because she was peering deep into Mr. Douglas's garage where he was measuring out a pole. "I thought he gave you the creeps?" she added.

I remembered back when Mr. Douglas used to stand in his garden and watch what I was doing, and I realized he didn't do that anymore. He was too busy building Champ's obstacles. "He's not that bad," I finally said. "Really. He's kind of nice."

"Are you sick, Riley? Have you gone mad?" Kaylee asked. She reached out and felt my head, pretending to check for a fever.

I knew Kaylee didn't mean anything by it, but I pushed her hand away a little harder than I needed to. "Mr. Douglas was right," I explained. "Champ needs something to do. Since I've been working with him, he doesn't bark as much and he doesn't rearrange things in the house, either. Besides, I like building stuff."

Kaylee thought about what I said for a full thirty seconds. She glanced at the obstacles spread over Mr. Douglas's yard and then reached down to rub Champ's ear between her fingers. "You really don't think Mr. Douglas is creepy anymore?" she asked.

I shook my head. "Once you get to know him, he's not bad at all."

"Well," she said slowly, "he did build some pretty neat things. I guess someone who doesn't mind spending his afternoons helping Champ can't be all bad."

"Exactly," I told her. "And Champ likes him, too."

"I told the rest of the team what you and Champ are doing," Kaylee told me. "They think it's pretty cool."

"Really?" I asked. I had spent my life in the shadow of my dad, the king of cool. Never, in all my life, had anybody used that word to describe me.

Kaylee nodded. "Not as cool as me, the home-run star, of course," she said with a grin. "But cool."

After Kaylee left for practice, Mr. Douglas and I spent an hour pounding old fence stakes into the ground to form weave poles. Dogs were supposed to zigzag their way through them. It didn't look that hard to me, but the library book said it was one of the most challenging obstacles for a dog. I guess the book was right. I led Champ in and out of the poles three times, gently holding his collar and going slow since it was hard for him to change directions. "Weave," I said over and over, hoping he'd learn the new command. "Weave. Weave."

I liked the way Champ followed my every word, his head tilted up so he could see my eyes, his tail wagging.

After the third time, I kneeled on the ground and turned him to face the poles. "Ready? Set? WEAVE!" I let go of Champ's collar and started going in and out of the poles, hoping he would follow me. "Weave," I called over my shoulder. "Weave."

Mr. Douglas did what he did best. Watched. When I reached the end of the poles I heard him laugh. Champ had beaten me by running right past the weave poles, not giving them a second glance.

"He doesn't get it," I said. "Maybe he's not smart enough."

Mr. Douglas laughed even harder. "Oh, I don't think there is anything wrong with his intelligence. After all, he did figure out it's faster to go around the poles."

I started laughing, too. Mr. Douglas had a

point. Champ probably thought I was the dumb one for going in and out.

We were still laughing when Kaylee and Frank rode up the driveway on their bikes, mitts swinging from the handlebars. Frank was in another fifth-grade class, and we didn't hang out much at school.

"Missed you at practice," Frank said.

It sounded nice, hearing him say it, even though I wasn't sure if he really meant it.

"It's not too late to sign up," Frank added when I didn't say anything. "We could use another player. We were depending on you to play right field."

Right field was perfect for me since nobody usually hit a ball that far. "Thanks, but I have to take care of Champ," I told him. "I can't make it to all the practices."

"That's the first time I've ever heard of someone quitting a team before even starting!" Frank said. He was joking and didn't feel the need to say it quietly. His voice carried across the yard and floated in the open window over the kitchen sink.

"Shh," I hissed, but it was too late.

I glanced toward the house. My dad's shadow was framed in the kitchen window. I had seen him come home a while earlier, and I knew his routine. Ever since he'd offered to move the obstacles to our backyard, he hadn't said another word to me about it. He would park the car, nod hello to Mr. Douglas, then go inside. There, he stood at the kitchen sink, drinking a glass of milk and staring out the window. Watching.

"Neat," Frank said, glancing across the yard. "It looks like a miniature playground."

"It is," I said. "In a way. They're agility obstacles for dogs."

"It's like that contest they have every year at the Founders Day picnic," Kaylee added.

"I never said we were entering that," I said before Frank got the wrong idea. "We're just having fun."

Frank walked over and stood by the last of the weave poles. "Can your dog do any of this

106

stuff?" he asked. "I mean, with only three legs it must be hard."

"Sure he can," Mr. Douglas said. "Why don't you show him what Champ can do, Riley?"

"Yeah, let's see how this works," Frank added.

I got a very familiar feeling in the place beneath my belly button. It was the same feeling I got when I tried to make a basket, kick a goal, or swing at a ball. I knew what it was. A warning sign that I was about to be embarrassed.

Champ sat by my left knee, looking straight up at my face, waiting for me to do something. Anything. He didn't know the meaning of embarrassment. He just wanted to play. "Let's go, boy," I said without much energy.

If Champ could tell how I felt, he sure didn't show it. He hopped up, tail wagging, and headed for the beginning of the course.

"Go," I said, tossing a make-believe treat through the tunnel. Champ knew the drill by now. He scampered through the tunnel and then jumped through the tire and over the bars.

Kaylee whooped.

Frank whistled.

I had to admit, it sounded good to hear them cheer for Champ.

"Go, boy," I yelled, relaxing a bit as I ran to each obstacle. Champ followed me. His gait had grown easy and smooth over the last several weeks. It was easy for me to forget that he only had three legs until Champ reached the balance beam.

Champ started up the plank of wood that led to the beam. He was almost to the top when he slipped. I reached out and grabbed him around the chest, steadying him across the bridge that was made of a wooden plank. His weight felt solid and heavy against my shoulder. I didn't let go of him until he reached the grass again.

"Good boy," Kaylee said. She clapped her hands and Champ ran to her, accepting his reward of a good head scratch.

Frank didn't say so, but I could tell he was impressed that Champ had done as much as he did. I stood there, realizing that I wasn't embarrassed after all. In fact, I felt proud of my dog.

"What are the poles for?" Frank asked.

"Dogs are supposed to weave in and out of them," I explained. "For every one they miss, they lose points. I just got finished putting them in the ground. Champ hasn't had a chance to get the hang of it."

"Very impressive, Riley. Imagine what you could do if you put that much effort into baseball." The words came from across the fence.

I had been so busy showing the team what Champ could do that I hadn't seen Dad come outside. Now he stepped out from the shadows of Mr. Douglas's old garage.

Kaylee looked at her sneakers. Frank looked at my dad. Dad and Mr. Douglas looked at me. So did Champ.

Dad did his best to smile. "I heard Frank say you missed sign-ups. I could take you this afternoon. Get you registered. Then I'll help you catch up. I'm not bad at tossing a ball, you know. Of course, you might not have time to keep building these contraptions in Mr. Douglas's backyard," Dad added.

Mr. Douglas cleared his throat. "Whatever Riley chooses to do is fine by me. Of course, I haven't minded helping him build the obstacles. He's got a knack for building."

"Champ likes it, too," I added. "The exercise is just what he needed. Haven't you noticed? He's not barking as much, and he hasn't messed up anything in the house."

"Gives us all something to do in the afternoon," Mr. Douglas added. "Been trying to talk Riley into entering that competition next month."

"Not much can come of it," Dad said. "The dog can't win. Not the way he is."

It's not like Mr. Douglas hadn't heard it before. I had been telling him that just about every day. Still, I was surprised that he ignored Dad the same way he ignored me.

"Besides," Dad said, "you heard Frank. The team needs him. The team is more important than playing around with a dog."

I remember when Dad had said the same thing about my bridges. To the King of Cool, constructing toothpick bridges wasn't cool. Neither was building an obstacle course for my dog. Sports were. Dad had grown up playing ball. Football. Baseball. Basketball. Holding a ball and being on a team was second nature to him. I knew, to Dad, that nothing was as important as seeing his son be a player like he had been. Any kind of player. Whether I liked it or not.

"Baseball isn't as important as Champ," I said. My voice sounded as stiff as the boards I used to build the bridge that Champ had almost fallen off. "I'm not good at baseball, anyway, and everybody knows it."

"You can't spend all your time building a doggy playground, for Pete's sake," Dad sputtered.

Whenever a kid gets yelled at by a parent, there is an unsaid rule that everyone pretends it didn't happen. That's the way it was then. There was total silence in Mr. Douglas's backyard. For a full minute, everyone found something else to look at besides my dad and me. A minute doesn't sound like a long time, but when you're in trouble, it seems like a month.

"We'll discuss this later," Dad finally said. He

gave Mr. Douglas a nod before turning and marching back to the house.

"He'll come around, Riley," Mr. Douglas said.

Mr. Douglas obviously didn't know my dad as well as I did.

11
Caught in the Crossfire

That night we sat in the kitchen eating dinner. Mom, Dad, and me. Champ was curled up under the table so I could scratch his side with my sneaker. I had attacked my meat loaf and mashed potatoes as fast as I could, hoping to get out of there before anything was said about that afternoon. It didn't work.

"Soccer. Track. Now baseball. You can't keep quitting just because you're not the best player on the team," Dad said.

"I didn't quit," I mumbled. "I just haven't signed up yet."

"Riley's been busy," Mom told Dad. "He's done wonders with that dog. Haven't had one problem out of Champ lately." Then she turned to me.

"There's still time to sign up if you really want to, isn't there?"

"There's no such thing as too late," Dad answered for me. "A team depends on every player doing their part. They depended on you, Riley."

I could almost hear a pep band playing Dad's high school fight song to go along with his words.

I pushed my fork into the side of my mashed potato dam. Gravy spilled through the crushed wall and pooled to the center of my plate. "I'm too busy for baseball," I mumbled.

Dad pushed back his plate. That was never a good sign. It meant he believed what he had to say was more important than eating.

"You can't let building a playground for your dog interfere with everything," Dad said.

"We told Riley he had to take care of his dog, and that's exactly what he's doing," Mom said.

Dad glared at Mom. Mom stared back. If their eyes had been lasers, I would've been caught in the crossfire.

"I want you to stop wasting your time, Riley," Dad continued. "I'll get you signed up for baseball, but you have to give the team everything you've got. Is that understood?"

It wasn't a question I needed to answer. He expected me to understand it. Or else.

"Is that what you want to do, Riley?" Mom asked.

"Of course it is," Dad answered for me. "That's what all the practicing was about earlier in the season, wasn't it? You wanted to play baseball and I want to help you be the best you can be. It'll be fun, Riley, you and me practicing together."

Mom ignored Dad. "Do you still want to play baseball?" she asked me.

All my life I had wanted to do something to make Dad proud of me, and I didn't want him to be mad. That meant there was only one answer.

"I guess," I said to my mashed potatoes.

Dad reached across the table and squeezed my shoulder. "I'll go to the parks office during lunch tomorrow and sign you up."

The next day Mr. Douglas was where he had been every afternoon for the past three weeks: in the back of his garage. I didn't waste any time telling him the news. "I can't work with you any-more. I have to go to baseball practice," I said. "I'll help you take down all the equipment on Saturday."

Mr. Douglas rearranged a hammer on the peg-board that hung on the garage wall. "Well, now," he said, "baseball is a fine sport. You'll make a great player. But just because you're playing base-ball doesn't mean you have to give up on the agility competition. Even professionals do more than play baseball. It's a fact that Babe Ruth spent a lot of time on the golf course and Mickey Mantle wrote books."

"But I have to go to practices," I told Mr. Douglas. "Then there'll be all the games. I can't be in two places at once."

"That's true, but I'll be right here when you get done," Mr. Douglas said. "We can work with Champ then. Now scoot. Your team is waiting for you."

Champ was used to spending the afternoon running through obstacles. He didn't want to go inside and wait while I swung at baseballs.

When I opened the door to the porch to let him back in the house, he dodged as if he were playing keep-away.

"Inside," I urged, using my meanest voice.

Champ woofed and hunkered down, liking this new game. When I reached out to grab his collar, he hopped back, just out of reach.

I gave up my mean voice for a whining one. "Come on," I pleaded. "I'm going to be late."

"Why not take him with you?" Mr. Douglas called across the fence.

It didn't surprise me that he had been watching, but it did surprise me that I didn't care. I guess spending three weeks working side by side with Mr. Douglas had gotten me used to the idea that he always seemed to know what I was doing. I faced Mr. Douglas. "How could Champ keep up with my bike?" I asked.

"Go slow," Mr. Douglas said. "He'll keep up. You'd make that pup happy."

I looked back at my dog. Mr. Douglas was right and I knew it. Champ had proved he could do more than I ever imagined. Besides, if I made Champ go

117

in the house, he'd probably get mad and herd all my underwear right out the front door for the neighbors to see. "Are you sure you're up to this?" I asked my dog.

Champ wagged his tail. I guessed that meant yes. I left Mom a quick note on the kitchen counter telling her where Champ and I would be.

Before I pedaled down the driveway, I turned. Mr. Douglas stood there by himself. Watching, of course. It struck me for the first time how alone he was. I waved to him before I turned down the sidewalk and headed up the block.

Mr. Douglas was right. Champ followed me the entire way. When he fell behind, I'd steer my bike to the curb and wait for him to catch up.

Since Champ only had one front leg, he looked a little lopsided jogging up the sidewalk. He moved a lot easier and was much stronger than when I had brought him home from Dr. Fayette's, that's for sure. Running those obstacles was obviously doing more for Champ than keeping him from herding pillows and shoes. It was keeping him fit.

As we got closer to the ball field, I slowed even

more. I wasn't in a hurry to see the team. My stomach bunched up and I could hear my heart thud in my head. I knew the feeling well. Dread. I'd felt it almost every other time I'd shown up for a game. But today it was even worse, and I realized why when Champ swiped at my hand with his tongue.

For the first time, *all* the kids on the team were going to see Champ. They would see his three legs and they'd all remember how he got that way. How I had missed a ball and caused an accident that ended up ruining a show dog's career. If they thought long enough about it, they'd all realize that the last person they wanted on their team was me, Riley Walters.

"Hey, there's Riley!" Kaylee yelled as soon as she saw me ride up. "He brought Champ."

The rest of the kids turned. A dog on a field with a bunch of kids is like a magnet. As a group, they stepped toward me. And Champ. Then they all started talking at once.

"He's so friendly."

"Not stuck up like Mrs. Lerner."

"He hardly limps."

The dread slipped away. I guess kids can surprise you sometimes. Even bothersome kids like Erica. Today was one of those days.

"You should see how Riley trained him to go through tunnels," Frank said. "He's built an Olympics course for his dog in his neighbor's backyard, complete with jumps and balance beams and lots of other stuff. It's for the contest at the picnic this summer."

"I had help," I said, but the other kids didn't hear. They were too busy asking questions.

"What kind of tunnel?"

"How did you build the jumps?"

"Did you get to use a saw? My dad won't let me."

"How can Champ do those things?"

Champ went from kid to kid, letting each one scratch an ear or pat his back. Nobody seemed to notice he only had three legs. They just accepted him for what he was. A friendly dog with a sloppy lick. I couldn't help but feel proud at the way he was making friends so fast.

I had never been the center of attention before.

It felt kind of good. "I show Champ what he needs to do. Then we practice. He's quick to catch on — just not quick doing it."

They were still asking questions when Coach Johnson blew her whistle to start practice. I knew Coach because she was Luke's mom. She didn't seem to mind that I was late joining the team.

I didn't do any better than usual that day. Still swung through lots of empty air, but it didn't seem so bad. When the ball bounced past me, Champ would hop to it. Nobody seemed to mind that the balls were getting a little soggy.

By the end of practice, Champ had made friends with just about everyone. Even Coach Johnson. "Champ makes a good mascot," she said, patting his head. "Bring him anytime."

Mr. Douglas, true to his word, waited for me in his garage every day after practice. Champ ran the obstacles better and better, though he still wasn't fast enough to win any competition. He couldn't get the hang of three things no matter how many times we tried: the balance beam, the teeter-totter, and those blasted weave poles. They were as hard for him as hitting a home run was for me.

The balance beam and teeter-totter threw off his balance every time, but he was always willing to try them, and I was always there to keep him from falling. But Champ wouldn't even attempt the poles.

I would go in and out of the poles, showing him how to do it. Then, when I gave him his command, Champ skipped them all and ran for the tunnel instead.

"They're too close together," Frank said one afternoon when Kaylee and a couple of other kids followed me home after practice to watch.

"It's not normal for dogs to zigzag like that," Luke added, throwing a chew toy into the yard. Champ took off after it, not paying the least bit of attention to the weave poles. "It's darn near impossible for a three-legged dog to make those tight corners. Especially when he just wants to play."

Mr. Douglas stood at one end of the line of poles. I stood at the other. Frank leaned against

Mr. Douglas's garage, using the end of his bat for balance. Kaylee and Luke sat under the balance beam.

"The course takes discipline," Mr. Douglas said, almost to himself. "And effort."

"If they weren't so close together I bet he could do it," Frank said.

"Wouldn't meet with competition regulations," Mr. Douglas said.

Still, after all this time, Mr. Douglas hadn't given up on the idea of entering Champ in the contest at the fair. "Frank might be on to something," I said. "The opening game for the league is at the Founders Day picnic so we can't be in the competition, anyway. It wouldn't hurt to space the poles farther apart, just so Champ could get through them."

Mr. Douglas smiled. "Riley, I think you have a good point. The way to tackle a big problem is to start with simple steps. Let's give it a try."

Everyone pitched in to help pull out every other stake. The remaining poles left plenty of room for

Champ to maneuver. I grabbed Champ's chew toy and hid it behind my back with my left hand. With my right, I pointed to one end of the poles and gave him his command. "Weave," I said in my sternest voice. Champ looked at me, then darted between the first two poles.

"Good boy," Kaylee shouted.

"Go, go, go!" Frank yelled.

But they cheered too soon. After the second pole, Champ skirted around all the rest and loped over to Frank. I watched Champ sniff the end of Frank's bat, circling it like it was a big stick and he was waiting for Frank to throw it.

"He'll never get it," I said, throwing the chew toy to the ground. "Never. He'd rather circle Frank's bat than these poles sticking in the ground."

"That's because he likes people," Kaylee said.

"Maybe," Frank said slowly, "we can help."

"How can you help?" I blurted.

"Not me," Frank said. "We. The team. I have an idea."

And then he was gone, racing down the driveway on his bike.

12
True Teamwork

Champ woke me on Saturday morning by sticking his nose in my ear. I tried to hide under my pillow, but he pulled it off and dragged it halfway across the room.

"It's Saturday," I groaned. "I can sleep late today."

Champ looked at me and wagged his tail. He didn't care if it was the second Tuesday of next week. He was up and ready to go.

Saturday was chore day. I heard Mom running the vacuum in the den and Dad cleaning the bathroom. When I rolled out of bed, I stripped off the sheets. I stuffed dirty underwear and socks into the hamper. Champ followed me from room to room, acting like he was inspecting all my work, but when I headed down the steps for breakfast, Champ forgot all about me. He made his way straight to the back door and stood at attention. He pointed his nose at the doorknob and he growled. I'd never heard him growl before, except for when we played tug-of-war with a piece of rope. He looked over his shoulder at me, then faced the door again and barked.

"What is it?" I asked as I piled my dirty dishes in the dishwasher and then swiped a towel over the countertops.

Another growl vibrated deep in Champ's chest.

"What's wrong?" I asked.

I found out as soon as I opened the door and stepped out onto the porch.

There, clustered with Mr. Douglas in his back-yard, were Kaylee, Frank, and half of the baseball team. They grinned when they saw me.

"About time," Kaylee said. "We were about to get started without you."

"Trouble is, we need the dog," Frank added.

"Dog?" I repeated, only it was a question.

"You know," Frank said. "That three-legged

126

animal with the tail that keeps moving. Goes bow-wow."

Kaylee's grin stretched clear across her face. "We're going to help you get Champ through those weave poles," she said.

"It was your idea," Frank said. "You said it yourself. Champ'll run circles around people, but he just doesn't get the idea of going in and out of those poles. Well, we're going to be the weave poles. Human weave poles."

Before I could make sense out of what they were saying, the team members formed a line in front of Champ, their bats planted on the grass by their sides. That's when it dawned on me. They were going to guide Champ in and out of the obstacle they formed with their baseball bats.

I led Champ to the front of the line. He looked up at Frank and wagged his tail. I gave Champ his command. "Weave."

Champ looked at me as if I had kibble boogers coming out of my nose.

"Weave," I repeated.

Frank slapped his hand on his thigh and

Champ's ears lifted a full inch. He step-hopped to Frank for an ear scratch. Frank gently guided him between his bat and Luke's, who then led him through the next two bats. In and out, the team guided Champ through the weave poles made from their bats. I ran the length of the human obstacle, praising Champ each time he made it between two people.

Turning the tight corners was hard; Champ's balance was thrown by only having one front leg. He stumbled twice. Each time, I reached out a hand to steady him.

When Champ made it through the last bat, we all broke out in a cheer. Mr. Douglas yelled the loudest. Champ added a few barks to the noise. I whooped along with everyone, but my cheer stuck in my throat when I saw Dad. He leaned against our house, his arms crossed over his chest. I reached out to touch Champ's back and watched Dad push off from the house.

"Did you see that?" Frank asked my dad.

"Champ's going to get the hang of this yet," Luke said.

"It was all Riley's idea," Kaylee added. "He knew Champ would weave around our bats."

"A clever idea," Mr. Douglas said as he joined the rest of us. "Never would've thought of it myself."

Dad nodded. Just a quick dip of his head. "I saw it," he said. "That's really something. What I'd call true teamwork." For some reason, the feeling in my stomach matched the tightness in his voice.

The team's straight line had disintegrated and a few of them were trying out Champ's obstacles. Frank was walking across the dog walk and two other kids were hopping over the jump. They all had forgotten about my dad, but Dad hadn't forgotten about them. He was watching, and I knew something was bothering him. I could tell by the crease on his forehead.

Later, after the team had scattered to their houses and Mom had left for the grocery store, Champ and I went back to the house for lunch. Dad stood by the counter, waiting for me.

"Watched the team leave," Dad told me. It

made me mad, knowing he had been spying. At least Mr. Douglas stood out in plain sight, but Dad hid in the house, peeking out windows.

"Aren't you practicing baseball today?" Dad asked. Only it didn't sound like a question. It was more like an accusation.

I shrugged. Pulled open the refrigerator. "Time got away from us," I said. "Champ is doing so much better. It doesn't seem to bother him that he has only three legs. He's doing great, don't you think?"

I wanted him to admit that Champ wasn't a total loser. That he was doing better than anyone had thought he could. And I wanted my dad to admit that I had done a good job training Champ.

Dad reached out to scratch Champ's head. "He's healed up fine," Dad said with a nod. "I can tell he gets stronger every day. You've kept your end of the bargain about caring for him. Your mother and I both appreciate that, but I don't think you should distract the entire team with your doggy playground."

"They're not distracted," I said, trying to make

my voice sound normal instead of mad. "They were just helping."

"How do you expect them to win the opening game if they're spending practice time playing with your dog?" Dad asked. "You need to focus on what's important—the team. You want to be ready for the opening game at the Founders Day picnic, don't you? I can help you get ready. You and me. Practicing. We can turn you into a real asset to the team for the entire town to see!"

There it was. The real reason Dad was making such a big deal out of all this. He was afraid I'd embarrass him. Again.

I had never decided to actually enter Champ in the contest. Up until that very second, I only had been using the obstacles to keep Champ busy so he wouldn't chew up the furniture or herd rolls of toilet paper into the living room. But just then, something took root in my gut. Dad would probably call it stubbornness. Kaylee would call it dumb. I didn't have my own word for it, but I did know, then and there, I was entering Champ in the contest.

13
News Flash

I knew Dad thought I was going to quit the baseball team. I wasn't going to give him the satisfaction.

Every afternoon I went to practice and then hurried home to work with Champ. When I told Dr. Fayette why I was too busy to help at the office, he didn't mind a bit. He even wished Champ and me good luck.

Every day, more and more people came to Mr. Douglas's backyard to watch. Kids from the team. People from the neighborhood. Mom and her friends. I had to admit, it felt good when Mom clapped for Champ. I guess she was clapping for me, too.

If Dad got home early from work he would watch for a while, but he didn't say anything. Every once in a while he'd ask how ball practice was going or if I wanted him to give me a few pointers. I didn't tell him I was still swinging at air.

Unlike me, Champ was getting much better with practice. His coat was sleek; his muscles were strong. He acted more and more confident as he made his way through the obstacles. His steps were bold; his ears were up. He rarely hesitated except when he faced the teeter-totter and the weave poles. "It's almost as if Champ is showing off," I mentioned to Mr. Douglas.

Mr. Douglas nodded. "Remember his former life," Mr. Douglas said. "He's used to having an audience."

I guess word got out, because one Wednesday afternoon a reporter for the *Davenport Daily News* showed up in Mr. Douglas's backyard. He'd heard about Champ from Kevin's mother, who worked with the reporter's wife. That's how things in a small town work. Somebody says something to someone who tells somebody else. Pretty soon the whole town knows.

The reporter introduced himself as Billy Reynolds. He shook Mr. Douglas's hand, then stretched his hand toward me. I stared at him for five seconds before I realized he wanted to shake my hand, too.

"I understand you're training Mrs. Lerner's dog for the Founders Day agility competition," Billy said.

"He's my dog now," I said firmly. I wanted to make sure he got that part right.

Billy nodded. "I heard her dog was hurt in an accident. Tried to interview her about it yesterday, but she closed the door in my face. Said she was too busy to be interviewed, just like she was too busy to take care of a crippled dog, but it doesn't look like this dog needs nursing. Do you know how he lost his leg?"

Billy Reynolds had been talking a stream of words so long and smooth I didn't realize where he was heading until he asked the question.

"It must've been a bad accident. Do you know about it?" Billy urged when I stood there, my mouth opening and closing like a guppy's.

It didn't seem possible that a news reporter didn't have a clue about what happened to Champ.

Mr. Douglas cleared his throat. "The dog got hurt in a car accident," he answered for me. "There was too much damage to the bone and ligaments to save the leg, but Champ seems to handle only having three just fine. Riley here has been working with him every day. Champ is strong and healthy, thanks to him."

Billy Reynolds scribbled in a little notebook and didn't notice when Mr. Douglas reached out and squeezed my shoulder. The pressure of his hand was steady and strong. I turned to smile at him. My mom had been right all along. There was nothing weird about our neighbor. He was nice.

I was up and running the morning after the interview. I had a system by now. I threw on my clothes, washed my face, and brushed my hair over my forehead. Then I galloped down the steps and took Champ for a quick walk down the street and back, making sure to scoop the you-know-what. After that I threw his chewed-up knotted rope a couple of times for him to chase and filled his water and food bowls. Once he was set for the day, I grabbed a bowl of cereal for myself, then hightailed it upstairs to brush my teeth. It was timed to the nanosecond so I wouldn't be late for school.

That morning wasn't any different — until I raced back down to the kitchen. My sneakers squeaked to a stop on the linoleum when I saw Dad sitting at the table with the local paper spread out in front of him.

Mom snipped a few blooms off the African violet perched on the kitchen windowsill. Dad stared at the door as if he'd been waiting for hours for me to make an appearance. As soon as he knew he had my attention, he cleared his throat. It wasn't a good sign, especially since he wore that all-too-familiar crease between his eyes.

Dad pushed the paper across the table. The kitchen table is small so it only slid six inches, but it was enough for me to see the article on the front page of section two. Billy Reynolds's article.

Mom stepped over to glance over my shoulder. "It's a good picture," she said, and her smile showed me she meant it.

I looked down at the paper. A picture of me with my arm around Champ's neck stared back at me. **Davenport Boy and Dog Defy Odds**, the headline screamed. I let a small smile tickle the corners of my mouth. I liked the sound of it. It sounded daring and brave. Then I saw the line beneath the headline. **Baseball Team Sacrifices to Help**.

"I was afraid those obstacles would distract the team," Dad said.

"I didn't ask them to help," I said. Anger crept into my voice and I felt the tips of my ears burn.

"But you didn't tell them *not* to help," Dad pointed out.

"I don't have time," I told him. I tried to sound polite but I knew I wasn't very successful.

"Riley's right," Mom said. "He has to get to school. This can wait until later."

Dad looked at Mom. Mom looked at Dad. The silence felt heavy. I was going to be late, but I sat down, anyway. It's what Dad expected, and I didn't want Mom and Dad to fight. Champ made his way under the kitchen table and rested his chin on my thigh.

Mom sat down and reached across the table to put her hand on my arm. "I think it's great Riley and Mr. Douglas have been working together," she told Dad. "They've accomplished a lot."

Dad nodded. "But he needs to put things in perspective. There's a lot he can learn from being on a team and there's a lot I can teach him about the game. He's made a commitment. He can't just back out when things get tough."

"Baseball isn't everything," Mom argued. "He can do both."

Dad didn't answer right away. He acted like he was chewing on Mom's words to see how they tasted. I almost fell out of my chair when he finally said, "You're right. What Riley has accomplished with Champ is great. But I just want us all to face reality. There's no way Champ can win an agility contest, but Riley can be an asset to his baseball team."

They were talking as if I wasn't even in the room, and I had had enough.

"Maybe I can hit a ball," I said. "But here's a news flash. I'll never be a great athlete like you were. I'm no good at baseball, just like I'm no good at soccer or basketball or anything else that you care about." My voice was getting louder and louder, and I couldn't seem to do a thing about it. "I can't throw. I can't hit. I can't run. I can't shoot baskets. So just give up on me. I'll never be good enough for you."

Dad grabbed the rim of the table and blinked at every word as if they were hitting him in the face.

"Riley, don't say that," Mom said. "That's not what this is about."

I was done listening. When I pushed the chair away from the table, Champ stumbled back. He looked to me and whined. "That's exactly what this is about," I told Mom. "Dad wants me to be the sports superstar of Davenport, just like he was. Instead, Champ and I are nothing but a big embarrassment to him."

"That's not true," Dad said.

"Your father just wants to help," Mom added. "He wants to spend time with you. Tell him, Joe."

But I didn't wait for Dad to say anything. When I stormed out the door, Dad didn't bother following. It wasn't until I was halfway to school that I realized why he didn't try to stop me. There wasn't anything else for him to say.

Except, of course, that he agreed one hundred percent with what I'd said.

14
Mrs. Lerner's Dog

After Billy Reynolds's article was printed, more people came to hang out in Mr. Douglas's back-yard. Kids from school. Neighbors from down the street. Even a couple of teachers.

Champ loved all the ear scratches and belly rubs. Mr. Douglas liked telling everyone how we used levels and hammers and clamps to turn garage junk into a dog's jungle gym. Dad didn't say any-thing, but I was pretty sure he liked absolutely nothing about it. I could tell by the crease in his forehead. At least he hadn't said anything. In fact, he hadn't said another word about the team since that morning in the kitchen.

As for me, it all made me nervous. Now that I had committed Champ to entering the contest, I saw how clumsy a three-legged dog looked on the obstacle course. Every day I wanted to give up. Then I'd think about Dad. I knew he was just waiting for me to quit. That's when I'd grit my teeth, narrow my eyes, and try to figure out how to help Champ. And he needed help. A lot of help.

For one thing, Champ still kept slipping on the dog walk ramps and he refused to try the teeter-totter unless I was right there, one hand on his back. He'd sit right down at the start of the weave poles and wait until the baseball team lined up to guide him through.

"Who's doing the training?" Erica joked one afternoon. "The kid or the dog?"

"Seems like the dog's done a good job training all the kids," Mrs. Jackson from down the street said.

The jests were meant to be funny, but I didn't laugh. Neither did Dad.

And then, exactly one week after Billy Reynolds's article ran in the *Davenport Daily News*, Mrs. Lerner showed up. She pulled her huge SUV all the way up Mr. Douglas's driveway as if she owned the place. I looked at the bumper, expecting to see it crumpled and rusted where it had bashed into the tree, but there was no sign of the collision. Mrs. Lerner opened the door and slid to the ground. She waved the newspaper with Billy's article printed on the first page of section two.

A couple of kids from the team were guiding Champ through the poles. Mr. Douglas leaned against the fence to watch. Mrs. Lerner marched right into his backyard.

As soon as Champ made it past the last pole, I kneeled down to give him a hug. That's when Mrs. Lerner spoke.

"My dog is looking good," she said with a nod.

It was as if the entire world hiccuped. I tried to wrap my brain around her five simple words and found they weren't simple at all. Actually, it was just one word that stopped time. Her first one. MY.

Nobody said anything for a full fifteen seconds, the leaves on a nearby maple flapping the seconds away. It was Mr. Douglas who broke the silence. "Riley's done a fine job with Champ," he said.

When he spoke, everything started moving again. The line of baseball players wavered and broke. Kaylee tripped on one of the poles and nearly fell onto Frank. And at the mention of his name, Champ pulled away from my grasp and hop-stepped over to Mrs. Lerner, his tail wagging as if he had just seen a long-lost friend. Which, I guess if you think about it, he had.

Mrs. Lerner's eyes softened when Champ nosed her hand for a head scratch. She squatted down to rub the soft fur of Champ's ear. "I miss you, old boy," she said in a voice softer than I'd thought possible from her. "I never would've guessed that he could recover from losing a leg," she said to me.

I wanted to tell her "I told you so," but I knew better than to be rude to an adult.

Mrs. Lerner glanced around Mr. Douglas's backyard. "My, my," she said. "You've been busy."

Mr. Douglas stepped up. He was proud of the obstacle course and wasn't ashamed to admit it. He rambled on about how we built the obstacles, learning about them from library books. How we used junk he had stored in his garage. How we had worked with Champ every day. "He'll be ready in time for the Founders Day event," Mr. Douglas said with a nod. "All thanks to Riley."

"I see," she said, almost to herself. Then she turned and smiled right at me. "If Champ is able to compete in the agility show, then he's healthy enough to come home," she said, as if that made all the sense in the world.

I stared at her, not believing the words that had just come out of her mouth. "He's my dog," I sputtered. "You said you didn't want him."

Mrs. Lerner smiled as if nothing was wrong. "I've had three calls since this article came out. People love Champ's spirit and tenacity. They want their dogs bred to Champ now. After all, he's still a champion, even if he did lose that leg. Champ can bring top dollar for the kennel. I'm afraid I'll have to take him back."

Her words were like water flooding across the yard, threatening to drown me. I struggled to speak. "He's mine. You can't have him back."

"Riley's right," Kaylee said, stepping to my side. I felt stronger just knowing she was there.

"Riley practiced with Champ. He worked at the vet's after school to pay off the medical expenses. It's not fair for you to take him back."

"The kids have a point," Mr. Douglas said. His voice sounded way too calm considering some lady had just threatened to steal my dog. "Riley took care of Champ. He's been working hard to train him for that contest."

Mrs. Lerner looked at Mr. Douglas. Then she scratched Champ on the head, and it made me mad that Champ wagged his tail. "Have your day in the park," she finally said. "Enjoy it. Because as soon as the contest is over, I am taking my dog back."

We all watched as Mrs. Lerner turned and marched back to her SUV. She tossed the newspaper on the seat beside her, then climbed in and revved up the motor.

It was as if Mrs. Lerner had just declared the sky was purple and the grass polka-dotted. I wanted to run after her. I wanted to tell her there was no way I would give up Champ. But I didn't do anything. I couldn't. The lump lodged in my throat was too big.

15
A Losing Plan

"There must be something we can do," Frank sputtered.

Mr. Douglas was out of hearing distance, putting away tools in his garage. Kaylee, Frank, and I sat beneath the dog walk. Champ lay by my side, gnawing on a rawhide bone. I kept my hand on his back, as if I could hold him there forever. One by one, everyone else had left, not knowing what to say after Mrs. Lerner had made her announcement.

"Champ would be unhappy living in one of those kennels," Kaylee said. "How can Mrs. Lerner use him just for money? What kind of life is that for a dog?"

I flopped back on the grass and Champ hopped up on my chest to lick my chin. I didn't bother turning away. I let his tongue tickle my cheek and slurp in my ear.

"The whole idea of entering that contest was stupid," I said. "Stupid, stupid, stupid! Champ never stood a chance of winning. Now, thanks to Billy Reynolds's article, Mrs. Lerner wants her dog back."

"What are you going to do?" Frank asked.

I thought about how I had dealt with basketball and soccer. "I can quit, that's what I can do," I said, sitting up so fast Champ hopped away, thinking I was ready for a game of chase. But playing was the farthest thing from my mind.

"Quit?" Kaylee asked.

"We have to make Champ a loser. That's the way to convince Mrs. Lerner she doesn't want Champ back."

Kaylee looked at me as if I'd just sprouted broccoli out my nose. "You would do that to Champ?" she asked.

"No," I told her. "I would do that *for* Champ. If Champ ends up as a big embarrassment, people will stop offering money to Mrs. Lerner for breeding rights. After all, who wants a loser as the father of their show dogs?"

Frank shook his head. "You've worked hard. How could you not let Champ enter?"

Kaylee looked at Champ. "It just might work," she said. "But how do you convince Champ not to try?"

I looked at Champ. He was bred for competition. Winning was all he knew.

Champ sat up and wagged his tail. He'd be willing to practice from sunup to sundown. "I can't convince him not to try," I said, "but I can keep him from practicing."

"What about Mr. Douglas?" Frank asked. "What're you going to tell him?"

"Don't worry," I said. "I'll think of something."

The next day, Mr. Douglas was waiting for me, as usual. "I leveled the pole jump," he said. "I bet we can raise it another notch and Champ will make it just fine."

When we first started, we had laid the pole flat on the grass so all Champ had to do was step over it. In the last few weeks, we'd raised it two notches. It still wasn't as high as the other dogs his size could jump, but it was pretty impressive to see Champ sail over the bar as if it were nothing. Last week, I would've been anxious to dump my book bag, let Champ out of the kitchen, and hurry to see my dog try the higher bar. Today was different.

All day I had worried over what to tell Mr. Douglas. Now I was face-to-face with him and I still didn't have a plan.

"I can't practice," I said. Keeping my eyes on Mr. Douglas's chin made it easier to lie. Of course, having my eyes on his chin made it easy to see his frown, too. "I don't think it's fun anymore."

As soon as I said it, I knew it was a lie because my whole body, from my forehead to the pit of my stomach, sagged with disappointment.

"What about Champ?" Mr. Douglas asked. "He thinks it's fun."

I shrugged. "Well, I can't practice, that's all there is to it. I have something else I have to do."

"What's that?" Mr. Douglas asked. He didn't sound mean. Just curious.

I wasn't good at thinking on my feet. That's the only excuse for what I said next. "Baseball," I said. "The game's almost here. I have to double up on practice time just like Dad said."

"I see," Mr. Douglas said slowly, and I was afraid he'd seen straight through my lie. "Well, then. You be sure to take Champ with you. He needs the exercise, and he likes the attention."

I didn't look back as Champ and I headed down the driveway. I knew what I'd see if I did: Mr. Douglas watching me leave.

16
Mountains out of Molehills

As soon as I got to the field, Kaylee tossed me a mitt and Coach sent me to my usual spot. There was a rhythm to the way everybody reacted that came from spending so much time around one another. Standing out in right field, with plenty of time to think, I realized something. This was more than a team. These were friends.

"I need your help," I told Dad that night at dinner. He stopped buttering his roll and looked at me, one eyebrow raised higher than the other.

"I thought about what you said," I hurried on before anyone could say a word. "The team needs me to get better. I can only do that with practice. Lots of it."

I expected him to smile, slap me on the back or give me a high five. I was surprised when that familiar crease worried his forehead instead. "I'm glad to help," he said. "But what about the agility contest?"

"You were right about that, too," I said. I thought it would be hard to say, but once I got started, the lie came out fast and easy. "It's a waste of time."

The next day, I hurried home to give Champ a few minutes outside. Mr. Douglas was tinkering in his garage but he didn't bother coming outside to say hello like he had earlier in the week.

I remembered how Mr. Douglas had stood up for me. How he kept Billy Reynolds from knowing the whole truth and nothing but the truth. Mr. Douglas deserved an explanation. That's what my mom would say. But how could I make him understand why Champ had to lose? Not just lose the contest but make a fool of himself. And of me.

Champ wanted to go next door. I could tell by the way he looked toward the garage and wagged his tail, but I pulled him back to the house and pushed him inside.

Each day after that, when I rode toward the park, I made sure not to look back down the driveway. I knew Mr. Douglas would be watching. I didn't look at the gash in the tree as I zipped past it, either. I definitely didn't look at the windows of our house where Champ's nose would be pushing aside Mom's African violets so he could watch me through the glass. It seemed as if I couldn't look anyplace except straight ahead.

Champ did not like being home alone. That much was clear by the end of the week. It started out small. Nothing really worth mentioning, except that Dad made it into something big. A mountain out of a molehill is what Mom called it. I mean, everyone with a half-ounce of common sense knows that dogs like meat. Dad shouldn't have been surprised when Champ hopped up and stole his hamburger from his plate at dinner one night.

"Get that dog under control," Dad said, pushing back his chair like he might actually dive for the hamburger.

I tackled Champ, but he was too fast. He had already gobbled half the burger and the other half had been pulled from the bun. I grabbed it and held it out to Dad.

"Here you go," I said.

Dad put his hands on the table and glared at me.

"Riley!" Mom said before Dad could utter a word. "He can't eat that. It's got dog slobber all over it!" She took a deep breath and got up from the table. "There's extra in the kitchen. Let's not have a scene over dinner."

My thoughts exactly. And I'm sure the whole thing would've been forgotten except for one small problem.

Once we had all gone back to eating, Champ circled the table, tail wagging and tongue lolling out the side of his mouth. I patted my knee, hoping he'd settle by my feet. And he did, for a while. Just long enough for the whole family to fall back into the rhythm of eating dinner. Dad was talking about work, Mom nodding every once in a while. I was stuffing the last of my hamburger in my mouth, thinking ahead to when Dad and I would practice after dinner, when Champ decided he'd had enough sitting around. He reached up, grabbed the end of the tablecloth in his jaws, and took off running.

I grabbed my end of the tablecloth, but I wasn't fast enough.

Green beans and ketchup. Potatoes and salad. Glasses and dishes all crashed to the floor. And still, Champ didn't let go. I guess it was a big game of tug-of-war for him. He dragged the tablecloth, along with the remains of our dinner, out of the kitchen and halfway to the front door.

"Riley!" Dad bellowed as he grabbed for his milk. The milk tottered and then rolled off the table, right into Dad's lap. The words he uttered after that were some of the same words I wasn't allowed to say, but I knew better than to point that out.

"Riley!" Mom echoed, diving across the table to try to catch the jar of pickles before it crashed to the floor. Too late. The glass shattered and released a cloud of dill.

Mom forgot about the pickles. She reached

over and jerked the tablecloth so hard I felt it burn as it left my hands. One more jerk and Champ let go. Mom wadded up the tablecloth. She didn't yell, but yelling would've been better than the tight, measured words she said next. "Get that dog out of my sight. Now."

"I'm sorry," I said.

"Sorry?" Dad sputtered, still trying to sop up the spilled milk. "Sorry?"

Mom slapped the table, silencing both of us. "Nobody say another word," she said, once she was sure she had our attention. "Not one single word. I'm going to take a bath. A nice long bath. When I get out, this mess better be gone!"

It took me a solid hour to clean up. The tablecloth was ruined; a rip ran straight down the middle. Dad ended up eating a peanut-butter-and-jelly sandwich at the kitchen table. We both kept our mouths shut, knowing better than to disturb Mom's bath by arguing.

Mom spent the rest of the night pinching dead blooms off her African violets on the windowsills.

Messing with dinner wasn't Champ's only

problem. It seemed like every day he did something that got us both in trouble. I didn't care when he nudged all of my books off my desk. And I got pretty used to putting the pillows back on the right beds when I came home from school. For some reason, Champ liked to drag them all into the family room and pile them in front of the television. Which, when I thought about it, was a pretty good place to have a pile of pillows. So that wasn't a big deal.

But then Champ did something that was a big deal. A very big deal.

I came home after school and did the quick walk-around-the-yard thing with Champ. The sun was high in the sky and I felt summer on its way. Then I hopped on my bike and went to the park, just like I'd been doing every day since Mrs. Lerner dropped the bombshell on me.

The Founders Day opening game was less than a week away. So far, I had managed to strike out more times than I hit the ball, and I had developed the habit of dropping the ball every time it came my way out in right field. In other words, practicing hadn't been doing much good. Kaylee had decided to help me work on my swing that day after practice, so I was extra late getting home. I knew being late wasn't a problem since Mom and Dad met at the grocery store after work on Wednesdays.

When I finally got home, hot and sweaty and tired after swinging the bat a gazillion times, I tried to open the back door. It budged an inch but then stopped. Something was blocking the way. I pounded on the door. The only answer was a yip from Champ.

I had to get inside. That meant going through the front door. Unfortunately, my key only fit the back door and there was only one place for me to get a key to the front. Mr. Douglas. Mom had given him a spare in case there was ever an emergency. I figured this was an emergency.

I dreaded going next door. I thought I'd have to explain why I'd given up on the obstacles. I expected to see Mr. Douglas frowning and upset. But none of that happened. Mr. Douglas didn't seem mad at all. Or disappointed. He smiled when

I walked into the dusty shadows of his garage, where he had been organizing his tools on a pegboard.

"How's it going?" he asked, as if nothing was wrong.

I shrugged. "Not so good," I said. Then I explained about the back door.

"I'll get the key," was all he said.

There were no lectures. No angry words. He just went and got the key and then walked next door with me.

As soon as I opened the front door, I heard Champ's nails scrabbling across the linoleum and into the hallway. He was nothing but wiggles by the time he reached me, and I felt a twinge of guilt for leaving him alone so long. I traded a good head rub for a face-licking.

"Better check out the back door," Mr. Douglas reminded me.

Champ followed us down the hall and straight into the kitchen as if he didn't have a care in the world.

"What did you do?" I gasped when I saw why the door hadn't opened.

Champ barked, a happy little yip as if he was proud of his latest efforts. Obviously, it had taken a lot of work for Champ to tug, drag, and roll almost every one of Mom's African violets from the windowsills and pile them by the back door. A trail of dirt led from the dining room, through the kitchen, and ended in a mountain of dirt, broken stems, dying blooms, and shattered pots.

"What am I going to do?" I said. I forgot that Mr. Douglas was standing there, so I jumped when he answered.

"Clean it up," Mr. Douglas said as if it was as simple as sweeping up dirt with a broom.

"Mom will kill me. She'll absolutely kill me. She loves those plants more than anything."

Mr. Douglas reached out and put a hand on my shoulder. I remembered the last time he had done that and how I had made a promise to myself to make up for everything he'd done for me. But I had already let him down. Now, here he was, his hand on my shoulder again.

"But you didn't do it," Mr. Douglas pointed out.

Champ still looked up at me with those moist brown eyes, his tail sweeping side-to-side across the floor. It was then that I noticed his paws were layered with dirt. I fell down to my knees and hung my arm over Champ's back, letting my forehead sink into the fur on his shoulders. "Mom will blame me," I said. "So will Dad. He'll make me get rid of Champ. I just know he will."

"This is about more than plants, isn't it?" Mr. Douglas asked it so quietly that I almost didn't hear him.

That's when I let it all out. I sat there, in the middle of the kitchen floor, and told him why I went back to the baseball team. I told him how Dad never thought I was good enough because I was bad at sports. I explained that since I was so good at losing, I was training Champ to lose, too, by not letting him practice the obstacles.

"That way Mrs. Lerner won't want him back," I explained. "She'd be too embarrassed to have a loser of a dog. Dad never liked Champ, and now Mom will never forgive him. Not for this. As soon

161

as Mom and Dad find out Mrs. Lerner wants Champ, they'll make me give him back so fast, my head will spin."

Mr. Douglas sat on the nearest kitchen chair and didn't say a word. Just listened. When I was finished, he shook his head.

"That's some story," he said.

"It's not a story," I told him. "It's the honest truth. My dad hates me and he hates my dog."

The lines around Mr. Douglas's eyes seemed deeper and his shoulders were rounded in a slump. "Being a father is tough," he said.

I opened my mouth to argue, but he held up a hand to stop my words.

"Don't get me wrong. You have a right to your feelings, and I'm not making excuses for your father," he said. "I'm just calling it like I see it. Your father certainly doesn't hate you. Some men just don't know how to talk to kids. Don't realize that what was good for them isn't necessarily the best for their kids."

"You do," I said.

Half of Mr. Douglas's mouth smiled. Only half. "I didn't always. I've learned a few things, getting this old. Your dad will learn, too. But you have to help him, Riley, and I'm not so sure lying is the way to go about earning your dad's respect."

"I don't want his respect," I said, and even to my own ears the words sounded angry. "Not anymore."

Mr. Douglas nodded. "What about Champ? What's best for him?"

My fingers curled around the hair on Champ's chest and he turned to lick my cheek. "He's happy here. With me," I said. "I am doing what's best for Champ."

"Are you sure, Riley?" Mr. Douglas asked, and I couldn't help but notice that he looked at the heap of dirt and broken pottery piled at the door when he said it. "Absolutely sure? Is that why your dog just ruined your mother's plants?"

Mr. Douglas had me there. When I had spent more time with him, Champ didn't cause trouble, but lately he had been trouble with a capital T.

"Don't let what you want get in the way of what's right," Mr. Douglas said quietly.

"But I don't know what's right anymore," I said. "You tell me."

Mr. Douglas shook his head. "You have to figure that out on your own, Riley. Now, come on. Time to clean up this mess."

That's exactly what we were doing when Mom and Dad opened the back door.

17
Failure with a Capital F

Mom stepped through the back door, looked at the pile of broken pottery, and dropped her bag of groceries. She followed the trail of dirt leading to the dining room and to the living room.

She didn't yell. She didn't scream. Instead I heard her murmur over and over as she made her way back to the kitchen. "No, no, no."

Dad didn't move. He stood in the open door, hugging two bags of groceries. He looked from me to Mr. Douglas.

"The boy needed the front door key," Mr. Douglas said, explaining why he stood in the middle of our kitchen with a broom in his hand.

Dad nodded. Just a quick jerk of his head. "You've done more than enough. Thank you."

Then Dad moved aside so that Mr. Douglas could leave.

Once Mr. Douglas was gone, I felt like an island in the shadow of a rumbling volcano. Mom came back into the kitchen and plopped onto a chair. She sat there, not saying a word, for at least thirty seconds. Her hands held her head as if she were trying to keep it from exploding.

Champ sniffed her shoe, nosed her hand, and whined. Still, she sat there staring at the pile of dirt at my feet. Dad still held the bags of groceries. I gripped the dustpan to my chest like a shield. It was as if someone hit the pause button on a tape player. Champ was the only one moving. He went from Mom to Dad to me. I dropped one hand to his neck to hold him steady. Waiting.

"Do you know how long I've had those plants?" Mom finally asked. "Do you know what it took to keep them alive?"

I blinked. "I'm sorry, Mom. I'll buy you some more. I promise."

I had never seen my mom's eyes so angry. I knew she wanted to yell, but that wasn't Mom's style. "My mother gave me some of those violets," she said, her voice so low that even Champ lifted his ears to make sure he heard her. "They were some of the last things she gave me before she died!"

Dad dumped the groceries on the counter and stepped across the kitchen, putting his hands on Mom's shoulders. His touch stopped her words and she took a deep, shaky breath.

"The pillows. The tablecloth. The hamburgers," Dad said. "Now your mother's African violets. When is it going to stop, Riley? What else will your dog ruin?"

Boys aren't supposed to cry. At least, that's what Dad believed. But there wasn't a thing I could do about the tears leaking from the corners of my eyes. They rolled down my cheek and dripped off my chin onto Champ's back. Champ reached up and licked my face.

"He didn't mean any harm," I said. "I'll make sure it won't happen again."

Dad shook his head. "That's the problem, son," he said. "You can't make sure he stays out of trouble."

"I know you don't think I can do anything right," I said. "But I'll prove you wrong on this. I will."

Mom shook her head. "You spend all day in school and then you go to baseball practice. It's not fair to Champ, being cooped up in the house all day."

"You don't have time for a dog," Dad added as if he really cared. "It's okay that you chose base-ball over having a dog, but Champ needs someone who has time to spend with him. It's too much for you to juggle both."

That's when it hit me. My plan had backfired, big time. Keeping Champ from running obstacles was the worst thing I could've done. Now my hole was dug so deep I had no way of climbing out. Thanks to me, Champ was doomed. When Dad and Mom found out Mrs. Lerner was plan-ning to take him back, they would think it was the perfect solution. Perfect for them.

That night I lay in bed, staring at the ceiling. With Champ curled up beside me it was too hot for covers. My fingers caught in the hair behind his ears and he grunted in his sleep. I wondered if I was in any of his dreams.

Everything had gotten so jumbled up. No matter what I tried to do, it turned out to be the wrong thing. I was a failure with a capital F. There was just one difference. I was determined to fix this. No matter what it took.

The next morning, I called Kaylee. "I can't make practice," I told her.

"What do you mean you can't make it?" she asked. "You have to make it. Our first game is on Saturday."

I shook my head, even though I knew she couldn't see me. "I'm off the team," I said. "For good."

"But what about Champ?" she asked, her voice a sudden whisper. "What about the plan?"

"The plan is dead," I said, and I told her what I had decided to do after lying in bed staring at the ceiling all night long.

Kaylee was quiet for a few seconds. Then,

"Are you sure you want to do this, Riley?" she asked.

"As sure as the walls in my room are yellow," I told her.

"But you know what will happen if you go through with it," she said. "So why do it?"

"Because," I said simply, "it's the right thing to do."

18
Moment of Truth

"You can stop worrying about turning me into a baseball slugger," I told Dad the next morning as I was leaving for school. I kept my voice even and calm. "I'm quitting."

"Not again, Riley," Dad said, propping the back door open with his arm. "Come back here and let's talk about this."

I stood in the backyard and faced my dad. "You were right," I said. "Nobody likes a quitter."

The crease in Dad's forehead was deeper than ever. "If I'm right, then why are you quitting the baseball team?"

"Playing baseball made me quit something that was more important," I explained. "Working with Champ."

And then I told him what I had decided. "I'm entering Champ in the Founders Day agility competition. But don't worry. I don't expect you or Mom to come and watch us lose."

I didn't pick up a ball or bat or my mitt after that. I ignored Dad's sighs and head shakes and even his forehead crease. I spent as little time in the house as possible, which was very easy to do since Champ and I were back to running the obstacles in Mr. Douglas's backyard. All of it led up to the Founders Day competition.

Saturday came bright and sunny as if everything was right with the world. I was *not* excited. In fact, I was downright nervous. I don't know why I had the same kind of jitters I got before a game, since I already knew we didn't have a flea's chance of winning the agility competition.

I spent the morning of the competition making Champ's coat shine. I bathed him and brushed him and trimmed his toenails. Even with only three legs, I knew he'd look better than any dog there. Champ seemed to understand how important it was. He stood still, letting me pick out tangles and mats. Every once in a while he glanced over his shoulder at me, his eyes with that now familiar look. Trust.

I didn't ask Dad for a ride. I knew the last thing he wanted to do was watch his son enter a contest that couldn't be won. I rode over with Mr. Douglas instead. We got there in plenty of time. There was a long list of dogs running before Champ. I stood at the fence that circled the obstacles and watched along with a small crowd of people. Most of them had dogs of their own. Billy Reynolds was there, too, snapping pictures for the newspaper as the dogs ran the course. The obstacles were much more professional-looking than the ones we had built, but other than that they were the same. They were in a different order, but I knew that wouldn't bother Champ.

A black Labrador entered the ring. His owner gave the command and the dog took off. He hopped through the tire rings and scrambled up the balance beam. He darted between the weave poles without giving them a second thought, and finished the course so fast it seemed like it was over before it began. Then it was time for the next dog.

This one was smaller, a mixed breed that looked like a hairy beagle. They lowered the jumps two notches and then the dog was given the command to go. He ran so fast that he missed one of the weave poles, but even so, his score would surely beat Champ's.

"Nice dog," somebody said to me, and I nodded without looking up.

"Isn't that the dog that was in the paper?" someone else asked.

"Used to belong to Mrs. Lerner," somebody else said.

Mr. Douglas reached over and put his hand on my shoulder. I was getting used to the feel of that hand.

I dug my fingers into Champ's fur and tried not to listen to the people around me until I heard a familiar voice.

"Hey, Riley," Kaylee said, squeezing between Mr. Douglas and me.

"What are you doing here?" I asked. "Don't you need to be at the ball field?"

She smiled so big her eyes crinkled. "You didn't expect us to miss out on this, did you?"

"Us?" I asked.

I looked behind Mr. Douglas. There, dressed in uniform, was the entire baseball team. My friends had come to watch Champ compete.

I looked down at Champ and couldn't help but smile. He was having the time of his life. It was obvious from his wagging tail and because he started herding me around, his nose pressing the back of my sneakers, his body leaning against my legs. Mr. Douglas had been right. A dog like Champ needed to perform.

Then the announcer called our names. "Don't be scared," Kaylee said.

"Easy for you to say," I mumbled. All those weeks ago, I had set out to show Mrs. Lerner that Champ wasn't useless. Now was the moment of truth. I was ready to show the world.

I looked down at Champ. He wasn't nervous. He was ready to go.

The crowd grew silent when Champ and I approached the starting gate, but then Kaylee started clapping and the rest of the baseball team joined in. I gave them a grin. When Kaylee and the team had broken the silence, it brought the rest of the crowd back to life.

"That dog can't compete," somebody said.

"He'll never make the jumps," came another voice from the crowd.

"Aren't there rules against this?" someone else asked.

"They never should've let him enter," said a voice that immediately made me feel like I had swallowed shattered glass.

I searched the faces until I found the face that went with the voice. Mrs. Lerner.

She stood just a few feet from the judges' table. She reminded me of a vulture peering down from a cliff, waiting for her next meal to roll over and die. I knew why she had come. She was going to let Champ run the course, and then she expected me to hand him over to her.

Then I saw who stood behind her and I felt even worse.

Dad. Mom, too. Dad had his arm around Mom's waist. He looked around at the crowd, that crease a dark line on his forehead. He looked confused. As if he had just been poked awake from a nap. Mom chewed on the corner of her mouth. My heart felt like it had dropped to my stomach. As soon as Mrs. Lerner let it be known why she was here, Mom and Dad would find out, and I'm sure Dad would be only too happy to make me give Champ back. More than anything, I wanted to grab Champ and run far away from the park.

I saw Mr. Douglas then. He stood by the fence, apart from everyone else. He gave me a nod. It was time, and I knew I couldn't run away. Not now. Not from this.

I walked across the course to adjust the jump bar. I knew it wasn't regulation height for a dog Champ's size, but nobody argued when I lowered it.

I held Champ's face, looking deep into his eyes until I had his attention. "Good boy," I told him.

"You show them. You show everybody what you can do."

And then I gave him his command.

When Champ started for the tire jump the crowd was absolutely silent, and I imagined they were holding their breath just like I was. Until Champ cleared the tire, that is. Then the crowd erupted in a cheer that was led by the baseball team. Champ zipped through the tunnel. He sailed over the jump bar. He darted through the barrel.

He was doing it. Champ was actually doing it. With each obstacle the crowd yelled louder, urging Champ to go faster. I could tell by the way he held his head and waved his tail that Champ was having the time of his life.

I heard Kevin whooping and Kaylee started chanting, "Champ! Champ! Champ!"

The balance beam was next and I moved to spot him. Champ touched the yellow stripe at the bottom of the plank and made his way up the incline. I stood near, ready to steady him in case he slid, but he didn't need my help. Next came the teeter-totter. Tricky for any dog, especially one with only three legs.

Champ went up one side and when the board tipped from his weight I held out my hand, just in case, but Champ rode the board until it finished shifting. Then he scrambled down the other side.

We were nearing the end of the course. I knew he hadn't broken any speed records, but Champ was showing everyone that he could do what they thought was impossible. And he was loving every minute of it.

There was only one obstacle left. The weave poles.

Champ galloped toward them, his ears flapping and tail wagging. "Weave," I commanded.

Champ glanced over his shoulders at me before heading through the first two poles. He turned as if he meant to go through the next set, but instead, he hopped out to the side.

"Come," I said.

Champ obeyed and circled me as I led him back to the first pole.

"Weave," I said again.

Still, he wouldn't go through the poles.

The crowd had grown silent again, watching my struggle to get Champ to do what he didn't want to do.

Crowd murmurs burned in my ears. I looked to Mr. Douglas for help, and I was surprised to see Dad had moved closer. He stood, his hands curled over the top of the fence like he was ready to vault it.

I should've been happy that Champ was a failure so Mrs. Lerner wouldn't be so determined to snatch him away, but I wasn't. Then I heard someone in the crowd.

"He can't do it."

Can't. I hated that word. I gritted my teeth. Champ was not a failure and I was going to prove it to them all. He *could* do it.

"Weave," I said, with more determination than ever.

Suddenly, the crowd started to move. It parted, making way for Kaylee and the rest of the team.

Kaylee, Kevin, Luke, Frank. They were all there. Even Erica. They trotted onto the field and lined up by the poles, just like they had in Mr. Douglas's backyard.

Kaylee nodded. Kevin grinned. "Weave," I said again, this time with more confidence.

Kaylee slapped her thighs and Champ, always ready to play, headed her way. Kaylee guided him between two poles, which landed Champ right at Kevin's feet. Kevin scratched Champ's ears and sent him through the next two poles. And so it went. The team that I had deserted was guiding Champ, pole by pole, until he reached the very end.

The crowd grew louder with each pole Champ passed.

"He's doing it," a lady next to Mrs. Lerner called out. "He's actually doing it."

I heard it. I knew Mrs. Lerner heard it, too.

"Go, Champ!" Kaylee called from the end of the weave poles.

Kevin picked up her chant. Even Erica joined in. Soon, everyone in the crowd was chanting. I glanced up. Mr. Douglas was cheering, too.

"Champ! Champ! Champ!" they all yelled. It was better than any daydream I could've imagined.

181

Mrs. Lerner's mouth was pressed in a tight line, of course. Mom wasn't cheering, but I did see her smile. Dad wasn't even looking at my dog. Or me. He stared at the crowd behind him. The crease on his forehead was gone and for a moment I thought I saw him smile.

I took a breath, gave Champ his final command, and then waited for him to cross the finish line. When he did, Champ hopped up, placed his paw on my shoulder, and licked my face. Billy Reynolds caught the whole thing with his camera.

It was a perfect ending. Perfect. Even if Champ didn't win. He didn't, of course. A dog with three legs couldn't go fast enough to win. Besides that, if lowering the bars didn't automatically disqualify Champ from the start, having the baseball team help out surely did. But Champ didn't care whether he won or not, and, to be honest, I didn't, either.

A hand grasped my shoulder, and I looked up, smiling, expecting to see Mr. Douglas. It wasn't.

"You never gave up, Riley," Dad said. "Good job, son."

All my life I had dreamed of Dad saying those

very words. Now, here they were, floating in the air between us, but they didn't sound right in my ears.

"Thanks, Dad," I said, and in that instant I realized Mr. Douglas had been right all along. This wasn't about winning, and it had nothing to do with trying to make my dad proud. It was about Champ. I didn't care what anyone thought. I just wanted Champ to be happy. And to be mine. That was the honest-to-goodness truth.

I couldn't tell Dad that, though, because people crowded too close. Kaylee was there. So were Kevin and the rest of the team. Mr. Douglas slapped me on the shoulder, his eyes disappearing into wrinkles caused by a smile that stretched clear across his face. Mom made her way to stand by my side, too.

Billy Reynolds was everywhere, pushing the button on his camera as fast as he could. Everyone was talking at once, and Champ added his two cents' worth with a few barks.

When Mrs. Lerner pushed through the crowd, people stepped aside to give her plenty of room. She opened her mouth to speak, but I surprised everyone, even myself, when I spoke first. "I know you came to take Champ back, but you can't have him."

Billy Reynolds nearly dropped his camera. "You're taking the dog back?" he asked.

A few people in the crowd started talking but I didn't listen to what they had to say.

"Riley?" Dad asked, the uncertainty in his voice hanging heavy in the air. "What's going on?"

This was it. There was no turning back. "Now that other people see Champ's not useless, Mrs. Lerner wants Champ back," I explained in a rush. "But she can't have him. She gave him to me fair and square. Champ belongs with me."

Mrs. Lerner peered down her nose at me.

I didn't blink. "You don't really want Champ back," I added. "You just want to use him to make money."

"Riley," Mom gasped.

"It's true," I interrupted. I knew I was going to catch it later for being rude, but I didn't care. I looked my dad in the eye. "I know you and Mom think Champ is trouble. But I proved to you that I can take care of him, and I can keep him out of trouble. He hasn't done a thing since we've been running the obstacles again. He's my dog and I'm not giving him up. Ever."

Mrs. Lerner held up her hand. "Strong words from a boy," she said. "But you might as well give up, young man, because I aim to take what's mine. Your father is a reasonable man. I'm sure he will see it my way." She looked expectantly at my dad.

Dad didn't answer Mrs. Lerner. Instead, he turned to face me. "You knew this, Riley?" he asked me. "You knew this all along, but you still brought Champ here?"

I looked at Dad and nodded. "I had to. It was the right thing to do for Champ."

I knew Dad thought Mrs. Lerner was powerful enough to cause trouble for anyone who crossed her. I also knew that Mom and Dad were fed up with Champ's behavior. Neither one of us blinked. I reached down and touched Champ's back, waiting to hear what Dad would say. Finally, he took a breath and faced Mrs. Lerner.

"I'll tell you what I think. Riley never gave up

on that dog, even when there was nothing left to do but lose," Dad said. "He brought a whole team together just to prove the dog's worth. Champ is no quitter, and neither is my son. Riley proved it to everyone here. My son proved it to me. Riley is right. The dog belongs with him."

With the crowd pressing in and Billy Reynolds clicking away on his camera, there wasn't a thing Mrs. Lerner could do. She glared at Dad for a full ten seconds, and I was afraid she was planning ways to make life miserable for him. Then she turned and pushed her way back through the crowd.

My knees suddenly crumpled and I kneeled down next to Champ. "Good boy," I told him. "Good boy."

My dad leaned down beside us and gave Champ a scratch behind his ears. Champ gave my ear a swipe with his tongue and then he stretched over to lick my dad across the chin. I couldn't help but laugh.

That was the picture that Billy Reynolds published the next day in the newspaper. Champ licking my ear. Mom laughing with Kaylee and Mr. Douglas. Dad leaning behind me, his hand reaching for my shoulder.

Champ might not have brought a blue ribbon home, but there was no doubt in my mind. Champ and I were the biggest winners there.

About the Author

Marcia Thornton Jones is the author/coauthor of more than 120 books for children including *Godzilla Ate My Homework*, *Jack Frost*, and the series The Adventures of the Bailey School Kids, Ghostville Elementary, and The Bailey School Kids Jr. Chapter Books. Although she never had a dog like Champ, she has shared her home with many animals over the years, including a dog, hamster, rabbit, turtles, fish, and cats. She currently lives in Lexington, KY with her husband, Steve, two cats and a fish. For more information about Marcia, visit her Web site at www.MarciaTJones.com.